Forever Freed from Birth

Based on a real story

by

A. Saranagati

one source press

Invocation

Homage to Ramana Maharshi, who last walked on this earth many years ago yet whose luminosity has not diminished.

Light was all and all was Light—
*glorious, eternal, unwavering Light. From within
the Light a growing force arose that held me in
its current, yet I was not apart from it, or it apart
from me. In a flash, the force enlivened a physical
body, which was also composed solely of Light,
and filled it with the Light of pure awareness.*

*I drew no distinction between the body and
those bodies that touched it. Neither did I touch
nor was I being touched. I was simply awareness of touch. Every appearance, every movement mirrored me—the Light that could not be
seen for Its brightness. The movements of the
body were not distinct from the movement of the
things around it. All that was changing moved in
a singular, continuous dance that emanated from
the Light of pure awareness.*

*The body's senses interpreted its surround-
ings as a vacillating array of form, color, texture,*

*smell, sound and taste. Sounds were heard, yet I,
pure awareness, was not separate from them.*

*Sensations arose as external and internal
circumstances changed. The hint of a specific
scent as the lips were touched incited the mouth to
begin suckling. Learning in this way was instantaneous and spontaneous. Amid the ever-changing
reactions of the senses, I remained the glorious,
eternal, unwavering Light of awareness from
which every form and action sprang forth.*

*Other bodies made audible sounds, giving
distinction to things. Hearing a particular sound
time and again, the voice in the body mimicked it
and I, pure awareness, associated it with a form.
The bodies gave each form a name, distinguishing
it as independent from other forms. Names gave
rise to thought. Thoughts proliferated and formed
perceptions. And thus, the thinking mind came
into existence.*

*Other minds taught the mind that it was its
body and gave it a personal identity. They also
taught the mind-body that everything seen, tasted,
heard, touched and smelled was distinct and separate from it. Assuming this individualization to
be true, the mind-body limited its view from the
glorious, eternal, unwavering Light to the light
of day.*

A young, blind beggar was squatting at the end of a row of other mendicants when a man approached them and handed out coins. The others leaned toward the man, whereas the young beggar's posture did not change as he extended his long arm upward. Before reaching him, the almsgiver had given all of his coins and walked away. The young beggar's arm was still extended while the other beggars fingered their money and amused themselves in conversation. All of a sudden, his free hand grabbed hold of his begging hand, as though reprimanding it, and forcibly placed it on his lap. Within moments his composure changed from expectant to complacent.

Across the street, a young woman stood watching. She stared at the young beggar, becoming as motionless as he was. After a while, she turned to a fruit vendor and purchased an apple. Timidly, she crossed the street and stood in front of the beggar. Though her form blocked the searing morning sun from his face, he showed no sign of relief. As the other beggars began ambling toward her, she nervously concealed several coins beneath the apple and extended her hands.

"Please take this," she said in a whisper.

As though woken from a dream, the young beggar flinched, sat upright and accepted the offering. The young woman ran back to where she had been standing alongside the fruit stand. She continued watching the young beggar as he felt every curve of the apple. Then he began eating it with undivided attention, one bite at a time, in unbroken rhythm. When only the bare core of the apple remained, he paused for a moment and then tossed it into his mouth, swallowing it in a single gulp. Then he took a water pouch from the bag beside him and drank from it. With the acumen characteristic of nobility, he filled his cupped palm with water and rinsed his hands. From across the street, the young woman stood transfixed by his every movement. When he became motionless once again, she too appeared to have drifted into a timeless realm.

A week later, the young woman was standing beside the fruit stall when she noticed the young beggar's eyes glistening. She rushed across the street to find out what caused his sudden change of expression.

Standing before him, her face brightened and she said in a soft voice, "Like rain falling from a cloudless sky, tears flow from your sightless eyes and trickle over your serene smile. What pleasure could bring you such happiness?"

"It's not pleasure, Miss. It's who I am."

Confounded, she said, "You're a blind beggar boy."

"That's who you see," he replied calmly, "but that's not who I am."

With a quiver in her voice, she said, "I've noticed you squatting here in the same place, day after day, extending your open hand to each passerby. But when alone, you appear to ascend to a faraway place, the likes of which I've never experienced. Where do you go?"

"I don't go away. I come yet closer to where I am," he said. "Why have you been watching me?"

"Curiosity." She hesitated. "You are a contradiction to my brother, who is also blind. He is withdrawn and has anger toward our mother, who attends to his every need. Where is your mother?"

"I don't have one," he said dispassionately.

"What do you mean? Did she die? Who looks after you?"

"Other beggars feed me," he replied. "They also give me the things they no longer want and take what people give me."

"If I may be so bold as to say, you seem to have a keen intellect. But I don't imagine you've had any schooling. Who taught you?"

"I was born with an appetite for learning. People like you often talk to me about their beliefs, concerns or whatever is on their minds. They tell me I'm a good listener," he said.

"They have been my teachers."

"How old are you?" she asked, unabashed.

"I don't know for certain. But those who claim to have known me since I was a child tell me I'm either twenty-one or twenty-two years old."

"Twenty-one?" she questioned. "Why, I'm almost twenty-one." She was so surprised by his response that her words began muddling. "I've taken you to be . . . well, to be a boy."

Amused by her befuddlement, he laughed. "In your eyes, I am a boy who is blind . . . and in my eyes, you are a girl who wishes to see."

She touched his hand softly before whisking away.

Two days later, the girl returned and placed an apple on the boy's outstretched palm. As he ate, she told him that she'd pleaded with her brother to come with her, but he refused.

"I didn't expect anything different, since he is afraid to go outside, or even venture from his room." Her eyes widened, and her expression brightened. "Would you consider coming to our home?"

He shrugged his shoulders and replied, "The other beggars would be upset if I left here, even for a moment. They depend on the alms I receive."

When he finished eating, she knelt beside him and asked, "Have you always been happy?"

"I thought so, until a few years ago when I learned that I had not been in my previous lives."

"Previous lives?" she said, curious. "How did you learn about them?"

"One day while I was sitting here, I sensed something approach me, though I could not detect its breath. 'Who are you?' I asked.

"A voice that seemed to come from within me as well as from outside responded, 'I have come to answer the question that often confounds your serenity.'

"Surprised that this 'Seer' knew my innermost concern, I said, 'I was born into a formless world, yet I have been blessed by its boundlessness. I have no kindred, yet I am not separate from anyone. I have no material possessions, yet I have no desires. I find no pleasure in gratifying my senses, yet I am always happy. I have no faith in what can be defined, yet I trust all that is unknown. What purpose has this existence?'

"The Seer replied, 'To gain this knowledge, you will need to revisit several of your previous lives, though collectively they will amount to less than a drop of water in the ocean of your incarnations.'

"In the next moment, I left my body along with everything I had known. The world of form, of which I had no prior conception, suddenly appeared before me as though I had always known it."

In a tizzy, the girl interrupted him. "Just now as you were speaking, I had the most incredible premonition that if you tell me your past lives, I will be always happy, as you are!" She paused before asserting, "I yearn for nothing more."

"If your yearning is true, it will be so," he assured her. "That is certain. Nothing can prevent you from having lasting happiness."

Returning the next day, the girl saw a well-dressed elderly woman sitting on a wooden crate beside the blind boy. Sometimes the woman moaned, while other times she cried and her hands trembled. From time to time, the boy nodded or interjected a few words, but for the most part, he remained still. While he listened to her with unwavering attention, his begging hand extended to each passerby, as if it were detached from him.

When the woman's monologue subsided, her body relaxed. She sat motionless beside the boy for a few minutes before standing up. Then she bowed her head and hobbled away with the aid of a cane.

Without making a sound, the girl sat down on the crate in the woman's place.

"You have returned," said the boy.

"Yes!" she exclaimed. "Can you see me?"

He smiled but did not respond.

"I'm hoping you will tell me the first of your previous lives that you experienced," she said anxiously.

He nodded and began, "This is how it was . . . "

"My son was born on the Crest!" my father often boasted. The Crest was the auspicious day when the constellation depicting the god Phaetius positioned itself in the exact center of the night sky. Of all the gods, Phaetius was the most venerated, as he controlled the destiny of all creation. His strength, agility and candor were unsurpassable, though according to legend, he often defeated his opponents merely with his steady gaze.

For generations, Phaetius had been the deity of many in my clan. They believed I was sent directly from him as a boon for their devotion and treated me, his namesake, as if I were the god himself.

My relationships with my fellow clansmen were established long before I could comprehend them or learn what would be expected of me. Many of them shuddered and became weak with fear when I looked directly into their eyes. From their reactions, I learned the power of my gaze at an early age. I was still a child when my relatives began asking me for counsel and begging favors. Without knowing how to satisfy their requests, I stared at them, causing them to tremble. Moments later, they would thank me for transmitting an insight or granting a boon, though I had done nothing.

When I was eighteen years old, the patriarch of the clan died and a rift developed between those who held Phaetius as their god and those who did not. Their feud divided them into two groups—the disbelievers, who took control of the clan, and the believers, who were ousted. My father and two of my brothers were among those who fled while my uncle became the ruling patriarch of the victors. I remained with him because he had been my mentor during my adolescence. He always treated me as if I were his son, and I turned to him for guidance rather than my father, who treated me as if I were his father.

In the period that followed the upheaval, I learned that the renegades joined forces with a neighboring clan and were plotting to destroy us.

One day while I was riding through the countryside, I came upon one of my estranged brothers. He was so gaunt I barely recognized him.

"What brings you here?" he asked, as he cowered away from me.

"I have come this way by chance," I replied, dismounting from my horse and standing in front of him. "How have you come to be destitute? I was told that you and the other renegades had increased your forces and are planning to overthrow us."

"Renegades?" he said with a feeble laugh. "We were exiled because we disagreed with our uncle, your patriarch! How could we overthrow you? He's starving us to death."

"That can't be true," I mumbled, dumfounded by his accusations.

"How could *you*, our cherished godsend, not know this?" he scoffed, before turning to run off into the thicket.

I yelled, "How is our father?"

He stopped and looked back at me with contempt in his eyes. "He refuses to speak your name."

"Take me to him at once!" I demanded.

Intimidated by my gaze, my brother yelled, "Kill me! Kill me now. For if I take you there, you will kill them all."

I caught up to him and grabbed hold of his arm. "You have nothing to fear," I said. "I will not betray you."

Trembling, he consented to my request. I followed behind him while leading my horse. When we approached his encampment, it appeared deserted.

I stood in the center of the clearing and cried out, "I am

your son, your brother, your fellow clansman. I have come to serve you! Phaetius has not forsaken you."

"Don't taunt us with your words," said an angry voice from within the thicket. "You are one of them, not us."

I yelled back, "I was led to believe that you would betray us."

My father suddenly appeared, standing as still as the trees that surrounded him. I went before his emaciated form, which had diminished even in height. My eyes welled as I knelt at his feet. "Please forgive me, father."

I felt his hand on my head as he said, "It is those heathens who tricked you. We must destroy their evil seed, once and for all."

He touched my shoulder, prompting me to stand up, while my fellow clansmen gathered around us.

"Why have you not sought aid from the neighboring clans?" I asked.

"They won't let us near their territories," replied one of my cousins. "Your patriarch has threatened to kill them if they help us."

I lifted my father onto my horse and instructed the others to follow behind us. As I began walking, the others formed an asymmetrical column of stragglers who were attempting to support one another.

"This neighboring clan will offer us refuge," I assured them as we entered their territory. But while I was speaking, we were bombarded with stones. I told my clansmen to take refuge in the underbrush and wait while I proceeded alone to the clan's stronghold. As I made my way forward, I caught the stones that were hurled at me and threw them back at my assailants. Once inside the fortress, I spotted the patriarch of the clan and ran up to him before his guards could catch me.

"You must feed and tend to the needs of my people!" I ordered, staring into his eyes. He attempted to speak but stammered and nodded, acquiescing to my demand.

During the days that my clansmen were convalescing under the care of our neighbors, a relationship developed between the two clans that melded them into one. With great devotion, our hosting clan took Phaetius as their patron god and turned to me for counsel, while my clansmen pledged their allegiance to their patriarch.

The united clan was celebrating the annual Crest when word came that my uncle was preparing to attack us. The governing patriarch and my father came to me and pleaded. "You must organize us into an army and lead us into battle."

"We can't fight them!" I exclaimed. "They are our fellow clansmen . . . our family. I will go to them at once and put an end to this madness."

"If you go, they will capture you," said my father, "and we will be slaughtered."

"Have you forgotten who I am?" I asked, looking intently into his eyes. He shuddered when I said, "Trust that I will return."

Upon entering the fortress of my uncle, I was seized by his guards. When my uncle saw me, he yelled, "Release him at once!"

Pulling away from the guards, I went before him. "You lied to me," I said. "Our clansmen did not flee. They were exiled, and now you intend to kill them!"

We glared at each other. My uncle was one of the few clansmen who was unaffected by my gaze.

"How can you initiate a battle against your own uncles, brothers, nephews . . . even one of your sons?" I questioned.

"Had our clan fallen to their rule, we would have been forced to take Phaetius as our god," he said. "They will always be a threat to our freedom because of their prejudice."

"Surely, you can reason with them and reach a resolution," I responded.

"It's too late for that," he said. "The trust between us

has been broken and new loyalties have been formed. Their alliance with the neighboring clan will give them a force much greater than ours. If we hesitate to act now, we will be destroyed. Of that I am certain." With piercing eyes, he asked, "Are you with us . . . or them?"

"How can I choose one over the other? My heart cannot be divided," I said, holding his gaze. "I simply will not participate in this folly."

"You have no choice but to participate. If you join us, we will be the victors. If you join them, they will be. But if you stand back and do nothing, we will massacre each other, and there will be no victors. Then, only you—Phaetius, the controller of destiny—will remain . . . with our blood on your hands."

"Is that who I am?" I asked. "The controller of destiny?"

"Well, isn't it? Are you not Phaetius?"

"If I were him, I would not allow this battle to take place," I said. "But clearly, I have not that power."

"Your eyes are outside of you," he said in a gruff tone. "Do you not know that our destinies are interwoven and immutable? Your desire to change the course of yours is the cause of your confusion."

"How am I to act in accordance with my destiny when I don't know what it is?"

"If you give your trust to the unknown, this question will be answered," he said.

"Trusting in the unknown goes against my beliefs, my better judgment."

"You trust your beliefs?" he asked, mockingly. "Have they always served to your benefit?"

"Well, no," I said, hesitating. "Not always and certainly not in this moment. Whichever choice I make will be wrong."

"You have been led to believe you speak the truth, the word of Phaetius, because others have always turned to you in this way. But the unknown, which is where your words manifest, is also where truth is found." His voice steadied. "It is also the source of every action."

"How am I to attain a position of indifference when others seek my guidance?" I asked, perplexed.

"You have nothing to attain that you do not already have. You exist in this very moment, but you distance yourself from it by holding the past and the future as true. Floundering between the two, you are caught in states of angst, confusion and doubt. Can you find these transitory states in the eye of the moment?"

"No," I replied. "But if I were to renounce my beliefs and ideals as you are suggesting, I fear that I would lose my power . . . or, worse yet, become a martyr."

"Fear does not exist in the moment. Yet it binds you to the illusion that you are a separate being in control of your own destiny."

"Your words soothe my heart," I said, "but my mind continues to doubt them."

A guard ran before us and said to my uncle with a tone of urgency, "Sir! We are in need of your counsel for the battle tomorrow."

My uncle nodded to him. Then he turned to me and said, "Take food and rest now. We will meet here again at dawn."

I did not sleep that night but labored over one unanswerable question after the next. The more I tried to gain understanding, the more confused I became. Long before dawn, I stood waiting for the arrival of my uncle.

Upon approaching me, he asked, "Are you joining us?"

Though I hadn't come to a decision at that moment, an unforeseen force overtook me and I nodded.

I asked him, "Why do I feel trapped in something that is against my will?"

"Our destinies are determined by our past actions. They are not beholden to our acceptance or rejection," he replied.

"If we are merely victims of circumstance, not accountable for our actions, what prevents us from doing wrong?"

"You are making an assumption that free will guards you from that. But in reality, it is the catalyst for the continuous reenactment of your habits, fears and desires."

"Then what purpose has free will?" I asked.

"It serves no purpose," he replied flatly. "It only fosters the illusion of being separate from the whole."

I turned away from him and mumbled, "Without it, we would not have choice."

"Not exactly," he said. "We have one choice—to free ourselves from our endless cycles of cause and effect by surrendering our desire to control circumstances. The continuum then burns itself out and comes to an end, once and for all. But if we attempt to control circumstances, we substantiate the illusion. How can the fire die if we continually add wood to it?"

A guard approached us, leading two horses.

"Come," said my uncle. "Together we'll lead our fellow crusaders."

After mounting my horse, I asked him, "What exactly needs to be surrendered?"

"Desire," he said while drawing his horse near mine. "Relinquishing the desire to control circumstances means to be satisfied with whatever is given."

"But certainly you have a desire to be victorious in this battle. Don't you?" I asked smugly, thinking he had contradicted himself.

"What I have been given is beyond my understanding. Neither do I like nor dislike it. I accept it as it is without desire regarding the outcome . . . that is, without expectations or regrets."

Rising from the commotion of horses moving into formation, a cloud of dust gave a golden hue to the morning light that danced among the glistening swords and spears. Joining the others as they rode off, I alone was separate from them, since they were not laden with doubts. As we neared the neighboring territory, our pace slowed to a walk. We stopped just below the crest of a hill to take rest before staging the attack. I seized the opportunity to clear my doubts and asked my uncle, "How am I to distinguish between what is given and personal desire?"

"When your mind is still—free of thoughts—this question does not arise, yet your actions continue. By trusting in the unknown of that stillness, you are freed from everything to which you have given meaning and believe as true."

"I've placed my full trust in Phaetius," I said.

"Is that so?" he replied, taunting me. "Can you act from your own free will and surrender to his at the same time? If Phaetius granted you free will, he would be neither omnipotent nor omniscient because you would control your own destiny. On the other hand, if he did not grant it to you, his mandate would appear callous and unjust, like the situation you feel trapped in now."

Though I understood what he said, I had more questions but they did not come to mind. I released a deep sigh.

Aware of my turmoil, my uncle said with compassion,

"Imagine you are an actor. The script you have been given is already written and cannot be changed once the play begins. Even though your part may be incompatible with your beliefs and wishes, you are not bothered by it because you know that the part is not real. Similarly, if you realize you are not a separate individual while acting on the human stage, you will not have fear or despair, desire or regret."

I understood and nodded. Acknowledging my affirmation, he gestured for me to follow him to the front of the others. When we reached the crest of the hill, I saw my father's united clan in formation not far before us. My uncle bellowed a threatening war cry that was echoed by the others behind us. The force across the valley replicated the cry. As they began charging toward us, I imagined my father was leading my fellow clansmen.

If they see me, I thought, *they will become terrified and defenseless. I cannot let this happen.* I pulled back on my reins, and my horse stopped dead in its tracks while the others passed by me in a flurry. Within moments, the opposing forces collided in an explosion of clamoring pandemonium. When the dust settled before me, I realized my uncle's prophecy had come true. From within the lifeless hush of the battlefield, the Seer said,

The mind is infinitely wondrous. It is eternal knowing without beginning or end and lies beyond the scope of words or concepts. However, it goes unnoticed when that which gives voice to it is believed to be real. This voice, which identifies itself as "I", "me" and "mine", colors the truth with latent tendencies, fears and perceptions that it holds fast in its memory. Without these illusive phantoms, the voice does not exist, and truth alone is realized. A still mind is eternal knowing.

When the boy finished telling his past life, the two sat without speaking. Occasionally the girl sighed, as though deep in thought, and swayed back and forth, causing the crate to creak.

Abruptly, she stopped moving and said, "It was your destiny not to join either side. But, if I understand correctly, had you taken the counsel of your uncle and surrendered your free will, you would have been freed from the endless cycles of cause and effect."

He nodded.

She touched his hand and scurried away without saying another word.

Upon returning the next day, the girl saw a middle-aged man sitting on the crate beside the boy. From the man's expression and gestures, he appeared to be talking about something of grave importance. At one point, his shoulders dropped as though a weight had been lifted from them. Then he stood up, gave the boy some coins and walked away.

Without making a sound, the girl quickly took his place on the crate. "Your uncle told you that you distanced yourself from the moment by holding the past and future to be true," she said hurriedly and then paused. "I imagined I had been living in the present. But noticing my tendencies after I left you yesterday, I began to doubt that assumption. What does it mean to live in the present moment?"

As he answered her question, his words seemed to flow through him rather than from him. "In the present moment, neither the past nor the future exists. Because of this, the moment is void of likes or dislikes, fears or doubts. The present moment is where we always are, who we never cease to be, and from which all actions originate. The present moment is the pinnacle of contentment and unity, holding not a trace of separateness. It is always accessible and complete in itself. While words and concepts cannot be found within the present moment, it is the essence of wisdom." He turned toward her. "If you are not in the present moment, who is?"

"Yes! Who is? Who am I? I never stay in the moment long enough to know because I pass through it like it doesn't even exist. Could I be afraid of it?" she asked, disturbed by her own question.

With compassion, he replied, "The past and future are creations of the imagination. They are erratic and ever changing, like clouds in the sky. Because we perceive them to be real, we give them our full attention and believe we can control them. On the other hand, we do not have this false sense of control within the present moment."

She bowed her head and said in a whisper, "I'll be back tomorrow."

When the girl returned the next day, several beggars were standing around the boy. One was giving him food and another was rummaging through his bag. When they left, the girl moved a crate alongside him and sat down.

"After leaving you yesterday, I attempted to stay in the moment. But all my efforts were in vain," she said solemnly. "I felt like I was in a boat with a hole in its hull, and water was pouring in faster than I could bail it out." Her voice suddenly enlivened. "As I was losing faith in myself, I began pausing every time I changed activities, such as combing my hair or washing dishes. I thought it a rather odd ritual, but I was curious about it, since it came to me of its own accord. During those pauses, my attention was not distracted by extraneous thoughts. As the day progressed, this ritual found its way into my every turn." Her voice rose. "I even paused before passing through doorways and before standing up from a chair or sitting down. In the midst of those pauses, I felt your presence, as though I was sitting beside you in a bright light." She smiled while reflecting on her experience. "In your blindness, I imagine you are always seeing this brightness. But in my brother's blindness, he only sees darkness. Why is this?"

He tilted his head slightly and rotated his body ever so slowly. "When we love who we truly are, we only see Light," he said. "But if we distance ourselves from that, we only see darkness."

"Who am I?" she asked in a whisper.

"You are ever-present, eternal awareness—nothing more and nothing less." As he spoke, she closed her eyes and a subtle smile gave her face a rosy glow. "Your boundless knowledge is complete in itself, exceeding the limitations of the conceptual world along with its many languages. Your existence is not confined to the body."

Her eyes sprung open. "How did I lose sight of this?" she asked.

"After the body receives Light," he said, "it is entered by an illusive dark presence that claims the body to be itself. This presence is the voice in the mind and poses as the mastermind of the mind-body. It maintains its autonomy by masquerading as an individual, separate and distinct from everything outside of itself. It revises the knowledge of awareness to its personal liking, which is based on its perceptions, tendencies and fears. And to retain its control, it obscures awareness with its incessant monologue."

"An invisible monster, indeed!" she exclaimed. Her tone softened and she asked, "What was your next past life?"

He smiled. "I had many lives between the life I last told you and the one I am about to tell you, though I did not relive them." He shifted his position from squatting to sitting cross-legged on the ground and began, "This is how it was . . . "

As I was growing up, my grandmother often told me, "You were the most stubborn and feisty baby girl—constantly moving, exploring things, exerting your shameless will at every turn. I wondered from where you could have come to possess such ambition. Certainly not from your good-for-nothing parents."

"I've wondered the same, grandma, and desire nothing more than to return to wherever that is."

My grandmother continued to lament. "The confidence that once sparkled in your eyes has all but faded away. Now, you sit in front of this loom day and night, moving the shuttle back and forth, while your parents gallivant through town squandering the profits of your labors. They treat you like an animal, barely feeding you. How is it that you have not grown resentful in all these years and run away?"

"I feared that I would not find happiness anywhere because I don't believe it exists. Besides, where could I go? Who would take me in? Perhaps my fate would be far worse than this one. The wretchedness of my life is familiar to me, whereas the unknown is frightening," I said, lowering my eyes.

"Dear one, please don't turn your eyes away from mine when you speak!" she scolded me lovingly. "I'm an old wretch in the twilight of my life while you are a beautiful woman in the springtime of yours. I don't expect to see the dawn of the coming year. But before I go, I have one burning wish that only you can fulfill." She raised her voice. "Regain your courage and free yourself from this dungeon!"

The fervor in her voice must have rekindled my confidence. I nodded, consenting to her wish.

Appearing both relieved and delighted, she reached into her brassiere and pulled out a crumpled envelope. "I've

been carrying this with me for many years. It is enough money to get you on your way, and a note introducing you to the daughter of my childhood friend." She then explained in detail how to get to the distant town of her birthplace.

The following day, I finished the cloth I was weaving, packed my few possessions in a handbag and ran off toward the river, intent on following my grandmother's instructions. Upon arriving at the dock, I was told that the transit barge had already left but another would come the next day at the same time.

Fearing my parents would come looking for me, I hid beneath an overturned boat, which was sitting on the shore. In my haste, I neglected to bring food or water and had nothing other than the clothes I was wearing to stay warm. Shivering throughout the night, I did not close my eyes for a moment and dared not venture from my hiding place until the next day when I saw the transit barge being loaded with cargo. Anxiously, I straightened my clothing and tied my hair back in a knot. As I was climbing the steps to the gangplank, I became dizzy and fainted. The next thing I remember was lying on the ground and looking up at the many eyes peering down at me.

"It's the weaver's daughter," came a voice from within the gathering.

"Is their house the wooden one beside the foundry?" yelled a big man, standing in front of me.

"That's the one!" came a voice from behind him.

"I'll drop her there on my way home," he said, as he picked me up and carried me off to his oxcart. Though I was still dizzy and my twisted ankle was swelling, I struggled to free myself from his grip.

"I have half a mind to beat you, girl. I'm trying to help you, and you're fighting me every step of the way," the man said and continued to reprimand me.

After pulling his oxen to a halt in front of my parents'

house, he hollered out, "I've got your daughter here. Come take this ornery critter off my hands!"

The front door of the house flew open to an enraged expression on my mother's face. She ran to the oxcart, grabbed hold of my arm and yanked me into the house. Then she slammed the door without acknowledging the man. As he drove off, I heard him cursing at her.

"Running away, were you?" yelled my father. He took my bag and dumped its contents on the table. Spotting the envelope, he opened it and read the note.

"Why, you wicked old woman!" he exclaimed, turning to my grandmother. "You twisted her mind and plotted against me."

"You're the wicked one!" she echoed. "You'll burn in hell for abusing your daughter and treating her like a slave. She doesn't—" Before she could finish, he slapped her across the face with the back of his hand. She fell, hitting her head on the edge of the loom, and collapsed on the floor. Blood oozed from her mouth as she held me in a loving gaze. Though horrified, I found solace in her eyes.

My mother yelled at my father, "You killed your mother—your own mother!"

"I didn't kill her, your imbecile daughter killed her by trying to run away." He picked up a large sack and began stuffing my grandmother's diminutive body into it. Before walking out of the house, he held up the sack and snickered. "You'll be the one who burns in hell, old woman! Let's be off to your new home in the foundry furnace!" Those were my father's last words to his mother.

After he left, my mother clasped the doorknob and said with contempt in her eyes, "You'll never leave here again. This door will be locked day and night."

I wanted to end my life then and there. The one person who loved me and taught me everything I knew was gone forever, and I was left a prisoner. I cried throughout the night. But just before dawn, the courage I had known as

"The intellect is limited to the realm of relative knowledge. Consequently, it does not have the ability to understand absolute knowledge, which can only be realized through direct experience. The intellect is limited to conceptual understanding, whereas the absolute is not limited by anything."

"While walking here today, I imagined I would need to climb an enormous mountain to reach the happiness you have attained," said the girl, daunted. "But listening to you now, I am thinking the mountain does not even exist." She touched his hand, as had become her custom, and said, "I'll see you tomorrow."

The next day, she gave him an apple before sitting down on the crate. When he finished eating it, she asked him if he would tell her about his next life. He took the water pouch from his bag and drank from it. Then, he offered it to her. With delight, she drank from it as if she were drinking nectar. When she handed the water pouch back to him, he began by saying, "This is how it was . . . "

"Your mother warned me that you were born with an unearthly streak of anger that could cripple anyone who comes near it," said my cousin, standing before me. "You have used that dark force to intimidate people and build an empire for yourself. But now, alas, you must face the consequences of your despicable deeds."

"I can't go out there. They'll kill me. You must help me escape!" I pleaded, terrified.

My cousin stood unmoved. "You forget, I'm not beholden to you as they are. Can you hear the anger in their voices? They are demanding that you show yourself, so they can end their rage once and for all. No one can blame them for that. But in their shortsightedness, they think the only way to free themselves is to kill you."

"They are the ones to blame, not me!" I replied, trying to gain my cousin's support. "I've been a pawn in their game. After all, I helped them out of their pitiful situations by lending them money. Yet they continue to whine, wanting this and demanding that, while attempting to unload their troubles on me. My only defense is to keep them in their place. It's their ignorance alone that holds them to my command."

"Perhaps," replied my cousin without showing a trace of empathy. "But you taunt them by increasing your fees and making them cower to your unreasonable demands. You've filled them with your spiteful anger. Now, only your compassion can set them free. You must show them that you are not to be feared."

"Compassion? I cannot pardon those who give me cause to be angry," I balked. "And, as you just reminded me, I was born with this inclination. It's what I was given. Just as your bald head is what you have been given. . . . We had no choice in the matter."

"I can't imagine my bald head adversely affects the lives of others. Furthermore, I'm not my bald head anymore than you are an angry man. If I believed my bald head is who I am, I'd be miserable like you."

"If I'm not the angry man, then who am I?" I asked.

"Certainly not the compassionate one who is concerned about the welfare of others."

"Are you so sure? I happen to believe otherwise."

My cousin's remark spurred me to ask, "You know something that can save me, don't you? Counsel me and I will forever be indebted to you. And be assured that I will reward you handsomely."

He pondered my offer. When he looked into my eyes, I imagined he was seeing my very soul.

"First, you must go out there and tell them you want to make amends for your wrongdoings," he said. "Then, give each one of them a chance to express their grievances to you. As they speak, don't turn your eyes away from theirs or interrupt them."

"Are you suggesting that I be hypocritical? I cannot tolerate their banal behaviors," I replied, indignant.

He took hold of my hand and pressed it firmly onto the right side of my chest. "While they speak, direct all of your attention to this one spot."

"But my heart is on the other side," I said, confused.

"That is your physical heart, where emotions are roused by thoughts," he explained. "If your attention goes there, your anger will flare. The right side is the heart of knowledge, which is void of all of your false notions along with the emotions they bring."

Silence fell between us, as the roar from outside the room grew louder.

"When I focus my attention as you suggested, it immediately jumps back to the other side, and I feel the full force of my anger again," I said, challenging his instruction.

His head tilted back as he laughed. "The bloodthirsty mob waiting for you outside will not allow your attention to jump away, even for a moment. For if it does, you'll be a dead man."

"How did you come upon this knowledge?" I asked, wanting proof of his claim.

His posture relaxed. "Several years ago, I was thrown from my horse," he said. "A saintly woman came to my rescue and directed my attention in the manner I just described to you. In so doing, she saved my life."

Though his story did not convince me, his confidence alleviated my doubts. I followed him to the door.

With a glint in his eyes, he asked, "Are you ready?" He pointed at the door latch.

I nodded. When I stepped outside, I was blinded by the fiery eyes and torches that faced me. My assailants began moving toward me as their knives and hatchets glistened in the light. Unconsciously, I raised my arms straight up in the air and pleaded, "I surrender and beg your forgiveness. Come to me, one at a time, and allow me to rectify your grievances."

My plea seemed only to heighten their fury.

"You scoundrel! How could you ask us to trust you?" came an angry cry. "We have all stood before you many times and been subjected to your abuse. We refuse to be treated like your slaves any longer."

The others howled in agreement. Paralyzed with fear, I directed my full attention to the place on the right side of my chest, as my cousin advised.

One man stormed in front of me and yelled, "You killed my wife!" As he spoke, the others began forming a line behind him. "The last time I stood before you was the darkest moment of my life. My wife was terminally ill, and I did not have enough money to feed my family." He stood so close to me that I could feel his breath on my face as he ranted, but I looked directly into his eyes and did not flinch. "When I begged for your help, you laughed and said, 'How will you ever learn to support your family if you always run to me for mercy?'"

As his anger escalated, my attention sank more deeply into the right side of my chest. From within that mysterious place, I felt a presence that gave me a sense of peace and well-being.

"I told you," he said. "All of it, for your sake, not mine. Only then might you be free of your venomous tendencies."

I felt a stirring on the right side of my chest as he spoke that seemed to validate his words. Yet I feared being duped by his logic and shook my head.

"Very well," he said, placidly. "Perhaps you will be granted another chance someday."

As he walked away, the room darkened and the Seer said,

Derived from behavioral tendencies, past actions dictate the course of future actions. When the mind is still and single-focused, these tendencies, along with the one who possesses them, cease to exist. Who remains in their absence is the one who always exists. To know that one is to be that one. And to be that one is to know that one.

"Still my mind!" exclaimed the girl, as her voice climbed an octave. "Before meeting you, I never noticed that my mind jumps continuously from one thought to the next and from anything to everything. *This* must be the mountain I imagined. But it's even taller than I expected." She began muttering to herself. "How am I to quiet a mind that knows not quiet?"

"What is this you call mind?" asked the boy.

She pondered his question for a few moments before saying, "Thoughts . . . it seems to be just a stream of neverending thoughts."

"If you follow them, one after the next," he said, "your attention becomes entrapped in their movement. But if you redirect your attention to their source, their movement ceases and the mind becomes still, like the stillness found in the eye of a tornado."

"Who redirects my attention?"

"Awareness, which can be likened to the ever-present sky," he said with a glow on his face. "Awareness becomes aware of itself without the distraction of thoughts, which can be likened to the ever-changing clouds that float through the ever-present sky."

For a long while, the girl contemplated his response.

"Amazing!" she exclaimed with bright eyes. "My mind actually did become still . . . at least for these last few moments. But I felt like I was holding my breath, and then when I let go, my thoughts returned in full force."

"When your mind was free of thoughts, who remained?" he questioned.

Frowning, she replied, "No one . . . just emptiness."

"You mean you disappeared?" he asked with a jaunty tilt of his head.

"Well, no, not exactly," she replied. "But nothing remained. At least nothing that I know or can explain."

In a soft voice, he said, "No thing can be found because what remains cannot be detected by the physical senses. Nor does it conceptualize or use language. It is awareness, known only through the act of being aware, just as breath is known through the act of breathing. That 'nothing' is what you are seeking: unwavering happiness."

From her melodic intonations, she seemed to understand his explanation.

"I've noticed that when you speak the Seer's words your whole being changes. More than once, you seemed to disappear before my eyes," she said and then smiled. "You remain a mystery to me." In her next breath she asked, "How do you remember the Seer's words so precisely? I need to write them down after I leave you, so I won't forget them."

Grinning, he replied, "The Seer speaks the absolute truth, which is known within the innermost heart of all beings. Trust that it cannot be forgotten, and you will have no need to write it down."

The next day, the girl sat down beside the boy without making her presence known. She closed her eyes and remained silent for a long while before asking him if he would tell her his next life. He nodded and began, "This is how it was . . . "

"Sha-koi-na!" came a stern voice as I was shoved forward. Blindfolded and handcuffed, I was one of three captured pilots being led down a muddy road into which I sank deeper and deeper with each step.

"They'll kill us even if we answer their questions," whispered my comrade beside me. "Remember our pledge to remain silent."

As I trudged through the mud, the sequence of events leading to that moment kept replaying through my mind: The right engine of my fighter plane had been hit; somehow, one of my shoe straps got caught in the fuselage as I was about to eject. While dangling upside down in midair, I spoke to my plane. *You have taken me through forty-two successful missions, but now you must let me go!* Instantly my shoe strap broke, and I pulled the ripcord of my parachute in just enough time for me to land safely.

The memory abruptly stopped when the clang of a metal gate sounded behind me. I heard voices yelling commands that gave me no clue to their meanings. Moments later, a gush of warm air swept over my face as a door opened. I was taken by the arm and seated in a chair. My blindfold was removed, but I couldn't see anything other than the blinding lights pointed at my face.

"What is your name?" asked the interrogator with a forceful tone, which reminded me of my commanding officer.

I remained silent.

His voice grew louder as he articulated his words ever so slowly. "What is the location of your unit?"

When I didn't respond, he spoke to the guard beside me in their language. The guard refastened my blindfold and took me to another room where my blindfold and handcuffs were removed, and I was told to strip off my clothing. I wondered what wrong I had done to deserve such a fate. Reflecting on my life, I determined that my arrogance was the cause of this curse.

I was handed a thin blanket on entering a cell that held several dozen prisoners, who all seemed to be speaking different languages. My attention was drawn to an older prisoner, standing off by himself. He appeared like an island of serenity amid a turbulent sea of anxiety that the others were generating. With a wave of his hand, he called to me.

"Where are we?" I asked him, hoping we spoke the same language.

"In a concentration camp in the middle of nowhere," he said with a heavy accent.

"How long have you been here?" I asked.

"Could be weeks or even months. In this place, we have no way of discerning night from day," he replied.

A cold draft swept through the cell as its metal door opened. The others wrapped their blankets tightly around themselves and became silent. A bucket of food scraps was dumped in a heap on the ground and a tall pot was set beside it. When the cell door slammed shut, the captives scrambled for the remnants, fighting among themselves, and drank the liquid in the pot with their hands. Within moments, not a morsel of food remained in sight. Though I was starving, I was too stunned by the display to move.

The calm man, who hadn't moved either, said, "I tell them they need not surrender their self-dignity, yet they choose to be victims of their own fears. Systematically,

He grinned. "It's an invention of the future. Imagine an oxcart that is capable of flying high in the sky."

His answer seemed to spark more questions for her. "Do the same characters return from one lifetime to the next?" she asked. "Like the wise prisoner who saved your life in this one?"

"Many do, but usually in different roles. My mother in one of them happened to be my brother in another. But the wise one did not return. He was freed from birth."

Returning the next day, the girl sat beside the boy without speaking for a period of time, as had become her practice. Then she said, "When I am here, my mind does not wander, and it is peaceful. But the moment I leave, that peace of mind leaves me as well."

"Who leaves here?" he asked. "Make that your pursuit, and your mind will be still."

"I will," she said in a whisper, as her posture relaxed. "What was your next life?"

He tilted his head and slowly rotated his shoulders in a circular motion several times before beginning. "This is how it was . . ."

"We'll be living here," said my mother, as we entered the servants' quarters of the harem. "Now you must promise to behave yourself and forgo your arrogant ways," she

warned. "If you don't, we'll surely have to return to the hovel from which we came, despite your good father's finagling that made this possible."

I despised being treated as an inferior. Yet the thought of returning to the home in which I had been born was immeasurably worse. To my eyes, the servants' quarters were paradise, though barren compared to the quarters of the concubines, which we had passed along the way.

"We are chambermaids," said my mother. "Your responsibility will be to sweep and scrub all the floors in the harem. If you complete your work by the time the sultan's children finish their lessons each day, you will be allowed to join in their activities."

As my mother was speaking, a servant girl of my stature approached me. Before introducing herself, she raised her hands to her chest and opened her palms upwards, as was our social custom before addressing someone of equal or higher status. I gasped at the sight of her grotesquely disfigured hands and shrieked, "What is wrong with your hands?"

"Nothing," she said undaunted by my outburst. "This is the way they came, and they serve me well enough. Indeed, my hands are not beautiful like yours. But can we not be friends?"

Her composure and gentle voice set me at ease, and I revised my perception of her. I had never had a lasting friend, but in that moment, I was certain the girl standing before me would be nothing less.

"Come with me," she said with a song in her voice. "I want to introduce you to the others. They should be finished with their lessons now."

Of the fourteen children living in the harem, my new friend and I were the only two who hadn't been sired by the sultan. The eldest male was the prince, who would someday rule the province. In one year, he would no longer be allowed to live in the harem, as was the rule for male children on their sixteenth birthday.

During that year, the prince, my friend and I formed an inseparable friendship as we competed with the others in an endless array of contests, from academic to sporting events. When the contests were the design of the sultan, he awarded the winners with valuable prizes. I excelled among the girls but I did not challenge the boys, remembering my mother's instruction.

"Whenever we're on the same team, I'm confident we will be victorious," said the prince to me one day. I gloated at his acknowledgement. "I'm thinking it's your cleverness, or perhaps your tenacity that makes you a born champion."

"She has both, and beauty as well," interjected my friend, who took every opportunity to boost my confidence, as well as my status.

When the prince left the harem and took private quarters in the palace, I rarely saw him, and then only at a distance. But on the day of his twentieth birthday, I spotted him talking to my friend in the passageway alongside the harem. He held up something that sparkled in the light and then gave it to her. Accepting the gift, she bowed before leaving him. Watching the two of them together, I was crazed with jealousy that welled up within me with the force of an erupting volcano. I loved my friend yet despised her for having won his affection.

Later that day, she showed me the gift and confided, "He said that when he first saw this tiara among the traveling merchant's wares, he remembered me and was inspired to gift it to me on his birthday."

As I held up the tiara, I noticed that its asymmetrical arrangement of crystals was in the shape of a star. However, their placement had a celestial mystique that gave the star the appearance of being perfectly symmetrical. Entranced by the design, I asserted, "It is magnificent. I must have it!"

Appearing stunned by my request, my friend took hold

of the tiara and questioned. "Have it? You've won all of the sultan's prizes. What need could you have for this?"

"I will give you all the prizes I've won in exchange for it," I pleaded.

"But I have no desire for your prizes," she said.

Chaos suddenly ripped through the palace as someone yelled, "The northern kingdom has been sacked by a nomadic tribe!" People began running in every direction, while my friend and I stood clutching each other. She handed the tiara to me and said, "If this will bring you lasting happiness, I want you to have it."

Every able male of the kingdom followed the lead of the sultan as he set forth to join forces with the neighboring kingdom. The next day, we learned that the nomads fled when their warlord was killed. But during the attack, our sultan was injured and died on his way back to his kingdom.

When the young prince returned from the battle, he was quick to establish his rule. He gave his mother the authority to govern his harem and honored the neighboring sultan by selecting four of his daughters as his concubines. He then began selecting his ministers and advisors. During that time, he requested an audience with my friend and me. I had not been in his company for several years and barely recognized him when standing before him. He had grown tall and become even more gallant than I remembered. His commanding presence might have intimidated his subjects had it not been for his humility, which gained him their love and respect.

He addressed me, saying, "Your intelligence would be an invaluable asset to this kingdom. I would like you to be my confidant and counsel me while I am conferring with my courtiers. Do you accept?"

I was thrilled by his offer and nodded, while my friend appeared even more ecstatic than I.

Turning to her, he said, "Your serenity calms my

mind. I would like you to be my personal attendant and accompany me wherever I go throughout the day. Do you accept?"

As she shyly nodded, jealousy arose within me to proportions I could barely contain. I wanted to be the one who was always at his side, not just on occasion.

He continued talking to my friend. "When we are together, I would like you to wear the tiara I gifted you."

"But, sire, I gifted it to my friend," she said with delight while turning toward me. "It brings her much happiness."

"But I intended it for you!" he exclaimed. Then he looked at me. "If you place your happiness above that of others, how am I to trust your counsel? The tiara was not intended for your pleasure but to honor the virtues of your friend. Return it to her at once!" he demanded before abruptly walking away.

My friend looked at me with an outpouring of compassionate tears, but they could not douse the anger that was flaring within me. Whenever I saw her after that incident, I ignored her. For a long while, she continued to look upon me as her friend, but I denied her that friendship.

My estranged friend became the sultan's personal attendant, growing more radiant with every passing day, while I remained a chambermaid, growing more sullen.

The sultan's mother, my governess, disliked me because of my arrogance. When she was abusive to me, I felt like a caged animal and even considered escaping to the hovel in which I was born. In the evenings, I often sat in a corner of the servants' quarters and closed my eyes, hoping that when I opened them, my life would somehow be different. When I opened my eyes on one of those evenings, my estranged friend was sitting in front of me. Smiling, she handed me the tiara and said, "The sultan has given his consent! You may have the tiara, and the happiness you so desire."

"It won't bring me happiness," I stammered.

"But I thought—"

"So did I," I interjected before she could finish her sentence. "But I have learned happiness cannot be found outside of me . . . but neither do I find it within me. While your heart is pure, mine is too tainted with pride and jealousy to receive such grace."

"Beneath the appearances of which you speak, our hearts are the same," replied my friend lovingly. "It is only your perceptions that taint yours and, as you said, they change. But happiness does not."

While she spoke, my unfounded perceptions left me, as they had done the first time I met her, and I was reminded that the woman standing before me could be nothing less than a lasting friend. When I returned her smile, the forms around me disappeared and the Seer said,

All thoughts are created by a singular thought—the "I" thought—which is created by preferences and aversions, which are created by habitual tendencies, which are created by past actions. If the ever-changing "I" thought is mistaken to be ever-true, the ever-present reality cannot be realized.

When the boy finished speaking, the girl looked intently at him and asked, "Cannot be realized by *whom*?"

"The one who appears to be real but never existed," he replied. "Each thought that spins off from the 'I' thought is like a mirage. If the mirage is perceived to be real, its creator is validated. But if the mirage is seen as a mirage, it ceases to be real, along with its creator."

"From what you say, my life is nothing more than a dream," she said with a sigh. "So, why do I feel trapped in it?"

"Who feels trapped?"

"The one who feels guilt and shame," she said as her voice trembled. "I doubt whether I can ever be free of it because *my* story is real."

He remained silent.

Regaining her composure, she confided, "My brother was born two years after me, and my sister came three years after him. Before she was born, my father doted on me. But afterward, she became his favorite, the sunshine of his life. In his presence, I was jealous of her, but in his absence I too adored her. She was beautiful, like an angel, and had an endearing quality that made people happy.

"One summer afternoon when I was eight years old, my family went on a picnic in a meadow not far from our home. After we finished eating, my father stretched out on a blanket to take a nap while my mother packed up the basket. She instructed me to take my brother and sister to the river and play.

"When the three of us got to the river, I hoisted my sister onto my hip and waded into the water, which came waist-high on me. My brother grabbed hold of my sleeve and followed us. At one point, he let go of me and became disoriented. I called out to him, but he was frightened and began crying. I waded back to the edge of the river and sat my sister down on the bank before going after him. Just as I grabbed hold of his hand, I saw my mother running toward us. I could not imagine why she was screaming, until I turned and saw my sister floating downstream in the current. Within moments my father appeared. He dove into the water and frantically swam after her. It seemed like an eternity had passed before he returned with her in his arms and tears in his eyes.

"My father claimed I was the cause of her death, and my mother and brother believed him. Over time, I accepted the guilt along with the shame. After the accident, my father became abusive, particularly toward me. I tried to appease him but all my efforts were in vain. That was twelve years ago and I never recaptured the part of me that died with—" She gasped as she looked intently at the boy. "I can see by the expression on your face that I've troubled you! I've taken your sunshine as well."

Before the boy could respond, she ran off.

When the girl returned the next day, she did not approach the boy but watched him from the fruit stand across the street.

Several beggars were talking to him, but his attention was elsewhere. At one point, he sat up straight, pulled a comb out of his bag and combed his straight, black hair forward to touch his eyebrows. Continuing with the same exactness, he combed it back in the opposite direction. Next, he combed it all to one side of his head and then to the other before giving his head a quick shake, allowing the hairs to fall as they chose. After putting the comb back in his bag, he drifted off to the realm that seemed familiar to him.

For several days, the girl came and stood beside the fruit stand but never ventured across the street. During that time, the crate was not in sight. But on the fifth day, it returned. She interpreted its reappearance as an invitation to rejoin the boy. After sitting down on the crate, she made a cooing sound to announce her presence. He acknowledged her by nodding but remained silent.

"I saw that you were touched by my story. But you were not trapped in it because you knew it as only a story. Isn't that so?" she said. Though he didn't respond, she continued. "I thought my family was the keeper of the key that locked me in my story. But since I was last here, I've come to realize that they live their own stories and do not hold the key to mine. It is the other way around; I locked them into my story." She laughed, though the sounds she made were barely discernable. "How can this dreamer escape from her dream when that is all she knows?"

For a while, he sat motionless. Then, he said, "With patience, and a burning desire to let go of the illusion you imagine yourself to be, you will wake up. That is certain."

She gently rocked back and forth on the crate, which creaked to the rhythm of her pensive inflections. At one point, she stopped rocking and asked, "Why are you telling me your previous lives out of chronological order, and why only fragments of them? Had you relived only those parts?"

The boy sat up straight and said, "That *was* the sequence in which they occurred. The ways of the universe are not as we imagine them to be. Its arrangements of time and events appear random to us because they do not follow the rules of logic. Sometimes, I was born into a body, while other times, I entered it later and left well before it died."

"How does this happen without my knowing?" she questioned, appearing confused.

"When we enter a body, we not only take its form but also its memory, which holds its history, language and social customs. So we have no way of knowing that we had not inhabited it since birth. It just might have been that you entered the body of your father after your sister died and only later entered the newborn body of your sister. Anything is possible."

"Oh, my!" she exclaimed, as her eyebrows rose and she fixed her attention on the ground in front of her.

He continued, "We assume life begins at birth and ends at death, moving in a linear manner that follows the principles of logic. Relative knowledge is based on those principles, but absolute knowledge is not limited by them, or anything else."

Dumbfounded by his reply, she shook her head and asked in a hushed voice, "What is 'life'?"

After a few moments, he answered. "At birth, all bodies receive the same awareness, which is perfect and complete, and makes no distinction between itself and anything else."

"Then, who is making distinctions?"

"The illusion of individuality," he answered. "It's a figment, like a bubble, that contains the accumulation of tendencies of past lives. Figments readily transfer from one body to the next and repeat their tendencies, over and over again."

"You mean the one who I take myself to be is just a repetition of tendencies?"

The boy nodded.

"That explains something that always puzzled me," the girl said, tilting back on the crate. "My aunt has three daughters. I took care of each of them from the time they were born. Though their appearances were similar at birth, their personalities were entirely different." The girl frowned as she asked, "From where do these tendencies come?"

"They are habitual patterns of thinking and behaving that are perceived to be true. They originate as attachments to concepts, such as 'I am the body,' or 'I believe such and such,' or 'I like or dislike something,' or from actions, such as lying and cheating."

Frowning, she asked, "How does one free oneself from their endless cycles?"

"By seeking the source of tendencies as they arise," he said. "In so doing, their illusiveness is realized because, in reality, they do not exist. The experience is like waking up from a dream."

"Who wakes up?" she asked, raising her voice.

"No one. Who we are has never been asleep and who we thought we were has always been an illusion."

The girl began rocking back and forth on the crate when a beggar woman ran in front of her and yelled, "Go on now! You've been here too long. You keep him from his work!"

Startled, the girl jumped up and said, "I can't leave now!"

The woman lunged toward her and shook her fist at her. "Go on!" she yelled. "Get away from here!"

The girl gave a shrill cry and turned to the boy. "Help me!" But he didn't respond, as his attention was far from what was taking place in front of him.

The woman picked up a handful of dirt and threw it in the girl's face.

The girl sobbed and screamed, "No! I won't go." But the woman continued throwing dirt at her until she ran off. Then the woman picked up the crate and walked away.

As the boy was taking a drink from his water pouch the next day, he heard the beggar women bantering among themselves. Amid their gaiety, he heard a familiar laugh that was much louder than the others. Moments later, the girl swirled around him with laughter that had not a trace of inhibition. She set the crate that she was carrying beside him and sat down.

"What was amusing them?" he asked, curious.

"I gave them some of my clothing," she said cheerfully. "I had always considered myself a compassionate person. However, after leaving you yesterday, I felt compassion for others to a depth I never imagined possible. I also began observing my actions rather than condoning them, which has been my habit. It was as though my whole world shrank from its distant edges of the past and future to the immediate moment, and I experienced the lightness of being." She stopped speaking and gazed at the serene expression on the boy's face. Mirroring his expression, she took a deep breath and respectfully asked, "What was your next life?"

After a few moments, he rotated his shoulders several times in his customary manner and began. "This is how it was . . . "

"I just swam across the channel!" shouted a man, entering the crowded dining hall in which I was sitting.

Many cheered him and raised their mugs, acknowledging his achievement. But the man seated beside me yelled, "Well, I'll have you know that I swam across it in the spring when its current was twice as swift as now."

"Swimming doesn't prove your strength as much as felling a tree with a trunk broader than your shoulders," boasted another. "And I can do that in half the time it took you to cross the channel."

"Why do you all measure your worth by the strength

of your bodies?" asked the magistrate. "Will you be less a man when your muscles are old and weak? The mark of a man is measured by his wit. To prove mine, I challenge anyone in this room to a debate."

"Will you still have your wit when you're so feeble you can't even remember your own name?" chided a silver miner, jumping up from his chair across the room. "My wealth will survive all of your human frailties."

"Listen to you all bellowing hot air about what you think is the measure of a man," chimed in a chambermaid, as she was passing through the dining hall. "If you knew who you were, you wouldn't be so set on claiming to be who you're not."

"I suppose you know who you are!" retorted the miner.

"I'm not saying that. But just yesterday I spoke to a stranger in these parts who didn't need to prove himself because he knew exactly who he was."

"Missy, the flies in your eyes make you blind in the mind," snapped the magistrate.

Though I joined in the laughter of those around me, I sensed our merriment was only hiding our personal fears and doubts.

Like my father, I was a street worker whose job was to pave the city streets with cobblestones. This grueling work broke the back of many a man I met while I was growing up.

Recently, I had the good fortune of being advanced from a laborer to a supervising craftsman because of my ability to interlock cobbles in artistic patterns. Rather than dig and haul stones as I had done previously, I now directed the workers to do that. My father was one of them. Though I favored him by assigning him light work, he felt he should have been given the position and resented being subservient to me. His jealousy influenced my mother and siblings, who sided with him. While working, he made a habit of ridiculing me, which incited the other laborers to follow his example.

As the chambermaid spoke out that morning, I imagined she was talking directly to me because I had no understanding of who I was. If I had, I was certain my life would not be so agonizing. Before leaving the inn that morning, I asked her if she knew the whereabouts of the stranger to whom she had spoken.

She cocked her head and said, "I overheard him telling the innkeeper that he has a hut at the edge of the foothills." Her eyes circled around the ceiling before continuing. "And something about a place where the river comes down from the mountains."

As she spoke, I was overcome by an inescapable yearning to meet this man. I left the inn, saddled my horse and rode off in such haste that I failed to consider taking any provisions with me.

The sun was setting when I came upon a solitary hut sitting beside a near-dry riverbed. As I was dismounting from my horse, a man came out from the hut and asked, "What brings you to these parts?"

"I have been traveling and would like a night's lodging," I replied.

"You're welcome to stay here, though my comforts are few."

I followed him inside the hut, which was furnished with only a knee-high table that sat beside a wood stove.

"You can use my blanket tonight and sleep near the stove where you will be warm," he said.

"And you? What will keep you warm?" I asked, surprised by his generosity.

"I've grown accustomed to the cool nights. My clothing is all I need. Rest now while I prepare something for us to eat," he replied, as he wiped the tabletop that reflected the movement of his arm.

I imagined the smooth surface of the table resulted from being wiped so many times over the years. Then he scrubbed his cooking pot with a piece of jute until it too was mirror-bright. As I watched him prepare the meal, my surroundings and sense of time disappeared within the rhythm of his gentle movements. We ate without exchanging a word.

The next morning after eating breakfast, which was the same fare he served the night before, we went outside and stood together in front of the riverbed.

"Since I've been here," I said, "I feel at peace with myself, almost as though it were my very nature."

"Yes. That is true," he replied. "It is your nature."

"If that were so, why is it not present all the time? I mean . . . when I am not here?"

Looking at the trickle of water flowing in the riverbed, he said, "It is always present, but your thoughts keep you from it."

"What do you mean?" I asked, perplexed.

"By habitually following after each passing thought, you have lost sight of your true nature, which is only present in their absence."

I contemplated what he said before asking, "But I'm never without my thoughts . . . am I?"

He abruptly grabbed hold of my shirtsleeve and pulled me backward. "Be careful not to get too close to the raging river," he warned. "For if you fall into it, its current will surely sweep you away."

I laughed, saying, "We're not in danger. It's barely a trickle of water. You're only imagining it is a raging river!"

"And you? Are you not imagining that you experience peace of mind only when you are here? Does it ever leave you? If so, could there be two of you—one who remains here and one who leaves?"

As he spoke, his words seemed to confirm something I already knew yet never acknowledged. I looked down at the crumbling riverbank on which we were standing and said, "If this raging river continues to eat the riverbank away, it will soon take your hut with it. We could fortify the bank by building a retaining wall with those boulders over there in the middle of the riverbed." I pointed toward them. "When I return, we will do just that."

He smiled and gave me an affirming nod.

As I rode away, the serenity I had been experiencing carried me home. But returning to work the next day, it left me without a trace of its memory. I began to doubt whether I was capable of truly being at peace and happy like the man who lived beside the river. *If I were a hermit like him,* I thought, *I wouldn't have any troubles either.*

Though my boss was pleased with my work and increased my wages, the workers were growing more contentious toward me each day. I imagined their sole aim was to reduce me to their rank again. In retaliation, I became an uncompromising taskmaster. I was not aware that my disposition had changed until the girl I was courting refused to see me anymore. She said I had become insensitive and arrogant.

One afternoon, my boss informed me that our next wagon-load of cobbles would be delayed because a bridge from the quarry was being fortified in anticipation of heavy winter rains. While he was speaking, I remembered my commitment to help the hermit stabilize the riverbank next to his hut. Since I wouldn't be working for several days, I packed my things that evening and left at dawn the next morning.

When I arrived at the hut, I found the hermit in the riverbed placing the final row of rocks on the retaining wall he had constructed.

Upon seeing me, he said with a whimsical expression on his face, "I wanted to get a start on the work."

I smiled although I felt guilty for not having come sooner.

Looking at his work, I said, "Your labors are commendable, but the wall could use some improvements."

He cocked his head and raised his eyebrows as if inviting my comments.

Walking in front of the wall, I pointed to its center. "This section is almost vertical. If the river current should dislodge one of these smaller rocks along the bottom row, the whole wall will fall apart, causing even more erosion." Kicking a rock at the base of the wall, I continued, "These boulders need to be twice their size, and they should be dug into the riverbed."

"From what you say, it appears I need to start again," the man said with a sigh.

"You've done the hard work already by lugging all these rocks here," I reassured him. "Now all we need to do is reassemble them."

For the remainder of the day, we dismantled the wall, segregating the rocks in piles according to size. At dusk, we finished the preparatory work.

"Come!" he said. "Let's wash up now in the stream. Then I'll prepare something for us to eat."

When we finished eating, I told him about the problems I was having with my family and work. While speaking, I noticed anger and anxiety arise within me as if I were facing those situations right then and there. He listened attentively without saying a word. When I finished speaking, he remained silent for a long time before asking, "Would you kindly repeat what you have told me so that I can better understand your predicament?"

As I was retelling my story, my emotions resurfaced again, but this time with less intensity, since the details of my story had changed somewhat. After I finished, we sat for a time without speaking. Then he said, "Please forgive me, but I need you to tell me your story again so that I can fully grasp the circumstances."

Though puzzled by his repeated request, I imagined he might have difficulty hearing, so I began again. But this time, my story changed even more, as well as my sentiments.

On his insistence, I retold him my situation yet again.

During my telling, I became aware that it was different each time. "You're making me repeat my story just so I can see the absurdity of it," I said. "Aren't you?"

"No," he calmly replied. "I wanted you to see for yourself that your thoughts and the emotions they elicit keep changing. With this insight, you realize they cannot possibly be true."

"I *did* see that!" I replied curtly, annoyed with myself for having botched my story. "My perceptions did keep changing." As I reflected on our conversation, I regained my composure and said, "But my mental state between each telling didn't change. It was like the calm between storms."

"Indeed, it was! So you *can* distinguish between you and the ever-changing, illusive you."

The next day, we carried boulders together and dug them into the riverbed to form the foundation of the wall. While we sat together after supper that night, I felt at peace with myself and with everything outside of me. Though it was a familiar feeling, I rarely experienced it.

I looked intently at the hermit. "Being here these past few days, I have come to realize that I am not my thoughts or perceptions. But I wonder how I can manage in the world without them. Must I be a hermit like you?" I asked, fearing that I would have to give up the world I knew to remain peaceful.

"Thoughts are not the problem," he replied. "They serve you in finding solutions and making decisions. It's your attachment to them that keeps you from knowing and being yourself."

"Are you saying I can let go of my thoughts at will?" I asked, dubious.

Nodding, he pensively stroked his beard. Then his eyes sparkled, and he began telling me a story:

"The king and queen had only one child—a son who uttered his first word on his first birthday. From then on, he spoke incessantly throughout the days, nights and even in his sleep. Those around him marveled at his rare intellect, believing he must be a demigod. His tutors were so impressed with his ability to speak and listen at the same time that several of them attempted to develop the skill. When he became the king, he gave higher ranks to those who succeeded in becoming incessant talkers.

"The next king also developed this verbal proficiency and, little by little, those in his court learned it as well. After several successive kings, almost everyone in the kingdom had learned the art of incessant talking, though few, if any, had mastered the ability to listen at the same time. Consequently, misunderstandings were commonplace, creating continual problems among the people. Those who did not develop the skill were considered ignorant and barred from the royal palace. Furthermore, as punishment, they were required to cover their ears with their hands when they were in public.

"It came to be that one crown prince refused to develop the skill and rarely spoke. Having no desire to become king, he ran away and lived in the forest. When the king was nearing his demise, he ordered three of his lords to find the prince and bring him back, since he was the only heir to the throne. The lords found the prince sitting beneath a tree in the forest and begged him to return.

"'Why should I return?' asked the prince. 'It is here in silence that I experience peace and happiness. If I were to become king, I would address only those who are silent in my presence, and no one would be allowed to speak in public.'

"When the lords returned to the palace and reported the terms the prince had requested, the king said, 'But incessant talking is our nature. Certainly he knows we cannot change who we are. Yet how can our kingdom survive without the leadership of a king?' Distressed by the quandary, he addressed the audience before him. 'I implore each of you to find a solution to this problem at once.'

"Amid the noise, the king's jester was the only one who heard his plea.

"'Have you forgotten about the ignorant ones, sire?' yelled the jester. 'They can act as our intermediaries.'

"The king rolled his eyes and began repeating, 'But they are ignorant.'

"'No more ignorant than the prince,' mocked the jester.

"Realizing the wisdom of the jester's words, the king conceded to his son's request. When the prince became king, the incessant talkers were not allowed to enter the royal palace. Furthermore, they were not allowed to appear in public without covering their mouths with their hands.

"After several successive kings, most everyone in the kingdom had developed the art of being silent."

I contemplated the hermit's story for a long while and then nodded. "It seems the only thing preventing me from being free from my thoughts are my thoughts. But how can I control them?"

"From one thought, the next arises, and from that one, the next, and so on," he replied. "You can stop this progression by directing your attention to where the thoughts are coming from rather than where they are going to. Their source is what you are seeking—where peace is found. When fully experienced, peace will never leave you."

The next day we continued to build the wall. When I called out for a particular rock, the hermit brought it to me and I dug it into the riverbank, interlocking it with the rocks around it. He worked hard to keep up with my pace and appeared to take pleasure in his participation. The harmony we developed while working together enabled us to complete half of the wall before the day ended.

While I was placing the final row of rocks on the top of the wall the next day, he surprised me by asking, "Why are you pushing me so hard?"

"Pushing you?" I asked, indignant. "I didn't realize you were having trouble keeping up with me."

"How would you know?" he snapped. "I am the one who has been lugging the rocks, not you!"

"If you had told me, I would have slowed my pace," I said, offended by his accusation.

"I see. Now you're putting the blame on me!"

Anger arose within me as we glared at each other. But when I caught sight of the glint in his eye, I realized he was taunting me. "You've tricked me again!" I exclaimed.

"So that you realize the importance of vigilance."

A short while later, I told him, "The anger that arose within me had a beginning, middle and end. At the midpoint, it overtook me like a wave and blinded me. But it passed away in only moments as I became aware of the one who was not affected by it."

While I was setting the last few rocks in place, I was still filled with doubt and asked, "How can I keep from drowning when I'm left to swim in an ocean of thoughts?"

"By fixing your attention on their source," he assured me. "Simple as that!"

I left early the next morning. As I was riding home, the bright morning sunshine suddenly darkened as the Seer said,

Like the surface of a lake, the mind moves in relation to influences outside of itself—interpreting, defining and evaluating its surroundings along with the physical body it claims as itself. Light shining upon the surface of the lake illuminates colors of every hue, like fanciful thoughts enliven the imagination. Ripples on the surface of the lake multiply while waxing and waning, like the interplay of desire and aversion causes thoughts to proliferate.

When the surface of the lake is without movement, its surroundings are indistinguishable from its mirrored reflection. Similarly, when the mind is still, the surrounding world is not seen as separate from oneself.

The lake is not its surface anymore than the mind is its thoughts. For if it were otherwise, peace would simply be a fleeting state of mind. To know the lake, one must dive deep below its surface. To experience everlasting peace, one must know that which exists in the absence of thought.

After the boy finished recounting his past life, the girl said, "I've been paying close attention to thoughts as they race through my mind. I had always believed they were essential for my existence, like the breath. But I am seeing they only keep me from being here in the present moment, which is existence . . . my true existence."

She mused while looking up at the sky, "When I follow my thoughts, I get lost in fantasy worlds, or memories that become increasingly more distorted, or things yet to come by rehearsing conversations and scheming ways to satisfy my wishes . . . even though I rarely act on those intentions." The tone of her voice lightened. "Why, just as I was crossing the street to come here today, I was thinking about a question I wanted to ask you. But as soon as I sat down, that question answered itself. The thinking mind did not give me that answer nor did it help me cross the street. Actually, it was a hindrance. It could only have been awareness that answered the question and brought me here."

"Yes," concurred the boy. "Awareness avails itself to you in each moment, whereas idle thoughts distract you from it."

"It should be easy to let go of thoughts rather than chase after them," she said, frowning. "But I get so entangled in them I don't even realize they are entanglements. For the most part, my thoughts seem to repeat the same nonsense that serves no purpose other than to take my attention and make me crazy." She sighed. "How am I to use my mind and be free of it at the same time?"

"The thinking mind performs a function that is intended to serve you, like a servant. If the road had been muddy, you would use the mind to plot a course across it. When you reached the other side, however, those navigational thoughts would no longer be needed because they finished serving you. So you let them go, allowing the mind to return to its natural state of stillness. But if you continue to hold onto those thoughts, they proliferate and the thinking mind becomes the master, rather than the servant."

"I understand," she said softly. She closed her eyes and sat for a long time without saying a word before touching his hand and leaving.

Upon returning the next day, the girl plopped herself on the crate. "I can't do this," she said while attempting to conceal the tremor in her voice. "Something keeps me from letting go of my stories."

She brushed away the tears that were running down her cheeks.

"Why these tears?" he asked with concern.

"Can you see them? Are you not blind after all?"

"I'm not blind to your feelings," he replied, lowering his voice.

When she began sniveling, he said reassuringly, "Children fall many times while learning to walk. Yet, due to their humility and faith, they eventually achieve their goal."

Her voice steadied and she said, "I've tried so hard to let go of the stories that control my life. But they have worn such a deep rut within me that I can no longer see above them."

"That too is only a story. Believing it to be true keeps you in its bondage." He extended his hand in front of her and clenched his fist so tightly that it caused his knuckles to turn white. "This is trying to do something," he said. Then he relaxed his hand, allowing his fingers to fall open freely. "This is surrender. Effort is not required to let go of idle thoughts. Yet trusting in that which exists in their absence requires great humility and faith. If you trust in that, you will be given guidance and confidence beyond your imagining."

"I would certainly welcome all the help I can get!" she exclaimed. Her face brightened. "I imagine you could have been an actor in your current life because you become a completely different person in each past life that you portray. Your voice, personality, mannerisms . . . everything about you changes."

"That is because I was them."

She laughed and then asked, "Who were you in your next life?"

He handed her his water pouch. When she returned it, he took several gulps and began, "This is how it was . . . "

"Your following has grown, since your last show here," the gallery owner said to me. "This is the most upscale crowd we've drawn in a long time. It's a numbers game—the higher the attendance, the greater our revenues. So invite your patrons back this Friday night for the preview reception of the remaining pieces of your current collection. And tell them to bring their friends. In addition to the food and wine that will be served, I've arranged for a string ensemble to perform."

I nodded and he walked away. Establishing a name for myself was important to me but, for some reason, it wasn't that night. If it were, I would have not only heeded his request but devised other ways to increase the numbers. Having studied the behavior of patrons during my previous ten shows, I noticed they were easily influenced by popular opinion and also more interested in 'being seen' and 'seeing who came to the event' than in my work. I learned how to win their favor by perfecting my flattery skills and becoming socially assertive.

"Wonderful show!" exclaimed my sister as she rushed up to me. "Your work has taken an upturn!"

"When did you arrive in town?" I asked, surprised to see her.

"I came this afternoon, but I need to leave tomorrow morning. I spoke to our brother an hour ago, and he told me about your show. It's serendipity that my brief visit coincides with your opening night."

"Will he also be coming?"

"I don't think so," she said wistfully.

"Has he had much success with his new book?" I asked.

"He didn't speak about it."

"Pity," I said with a sigh. "He's got so much talent, but he doesn't do anything with it. He needs to write for an audience rather than solely for his own pleasure. I've told him how to be successful, but he either doesn't hear me or ignores my advice."

"He hears you," she replied. "But he chooses to follow his creative passion. Between the three of us, our artistic journeys are quite different. When I perform the work of a composer who inspires me, I become so enraptured that I feel as if I were that composer himself. Ironically, my audiences credit me for the creativity of the music, when it's not mine. In a sense, I ride on the shirttails of the composers I revere."

"What do you mean? You are exceptionally creative."

She laughed, discounting his compliment. "Like our brother's books, the music I compose is rarely appreciated by others. While the lack of acknowledgement discourages me, he isn't bothered by it. His pleasure seems to come from writing from his heart to his heart."

"Do you know why he never acknowledges my sculptures or comes to my shows?" I asked, curious. "Do you think he's jealous of me?"

"I don't think he understands your work," she replied.

"What do you think of it?"

"These three new pieces of yours are masterful, as I'm certain our brother would agree," she said, and turned away, smiling. "Let's talk before I leave tomorrow."

A patron walked up to me and placed his hand on my shoulder as if he knew me. Then he gestured to a distinguished-looking gentleman, inviting him to join us. "I would like you to meet our senator," he said, introducing us. "The senator is impressed with your works and interested in purchasing one of them. Would you be willing to negotiate a price?"

Though annoyed by the patron's arrogance, I replied politely, "The gallery owner can do that."

"Yes, of course. But I thought you might want to facilitate the senator's request, as he intends to have the piece centrally placed in the foyer of the capitol building," the patron said, smugly.

Before excusing myself, I agreed to the price the senator offered.

Another patron caught my attention and led me to one of my current sculptures. "I've been an admirer of your work for years," she said. "But I must say that your three new pieces are a deviation from your style, which has always captured the elevating qualities of romance and nobility." She pointed at the sculpture in front of us. "The expressions on the faces of these two figures seem contrived and leave me feeling disturbed. What were you intending?"

"The mother is showing affection for her son," I said, groping for words, "though, at the same time, she is tormented by something he just told her."

As I was trying to substantiate the meaning of the sculpture to the patron, my words seemed to distance me from the experience I had while working it. However, her question prompted me to reflect upon that experience, which I had not done until that moment.

While creating each of the six pieces, I felt a force much greater than mine was forming them against my wishes. I was no longer the sculptor but a spectator. Though I was in awe of the mysterious force, I felt power-less and often became anxious. Sometimes, I struggled to regain my control, while other times I surrendered to the force, admiring its work. Upon completing the six pieces, I had no desire or motivation to continue sculpting.

"The child is smiling at his mother hoping to relieve her concerns," I said, though I was as perplexed by the piece as the patron.

She scrutinized the sculpture and then shook her head. "Very different," she said, forcing a smile.

An art critic interrupted us saying, "May I have a moment of your time? I'm writing an article about your show and would like to ask you a few questions before I leave."

I nodded to him, and the patron wandered off into the crowd.

He pulled a pen and notepad from his pocket and asked, "Were you born with this extraordinary creative talent?"

"On the contrary!" I exclaimed. "I had no creative inter-est during my childhood. My two siblings were born with talent, not I."

"Then, where did it come from?" he asked, appearing surprised by my response.

"My parents. They loved the arts and encouraged us in this way. Eminent artists, musicians and poets frequented our home. Though I had no artistic ambition, I was drawn to the tactile aspect of sculpting and pursued the art. But, in truth, I did it only to please my parents and rival my siblings."

"So . . . when did the creative passion arise within you?" he prodded.

"It never did," I said flippantly. "From the beginning, I saw it as a means to an end. I approached the craft academically, refining my abilities and mastering the techniques." As I responded, I imagined his questions might lead me to an understanding of my recent work. "I set my mind on perfecting my skills and won a scholarship to the National Art Institute. Upon graduating, my aim was to become successful in the eyes of my teachers and peers. So I developed a style that would appeal to the desires of art patrons."

"How would you describe your style?" he questioned.

"Predictable, sentimental and . . . repetitive."

"Repetitive?" he said, appearing disturbed by my reply.

"That's right, repetitive," I echoed. "Each of the faces of my figures has an altruistic yet melodramatic mien that is accentuated by an overall lack of expression. If you cover the eyes of any of them with your hand, you will see what I mean." As I was speaking, I had a sudden urge to do just that with my new pieces in hopes of finding their creator.

"I find it hard to believe that your sculptures are based on a formula. I imagined they were inspired from somewhere deep within you that touches the same spot within those viewing them."

"I aim for that spot," I replied cynically and laughed. "The *soft* spot that appeals to the fantasies and desires of viewers."

"Oh!" he said, looking at his watch. "I didn't realize it was so late. I need to leave. Thank you for your time."

The next morning I met my sister for breakfast at a restaurant near the train station. I told her about my loss of ambition and the experience I had while creating my recent works. "I approach sculpting methodically, executing the work in a linear manner from the beginning to the end. But this time, the finished image that I had in my mind's eye kept changing. Each time this happened, I needed to step back and redefine the piece. I found myself working in circular patterns that kept me from visualizing my destination. In the process, I lost myself and watched each piece take form on its own, without me."

She laughed, throwing her head back.

"What's so funny?" I asked.

"Ten years ago, our brother had the same experience you just described. I remember the childlike wonder in his eyes as he shared it with me. But you seem distressed by it."

After she boarded the train, I went to my art studio and stood in the center of the room. My attention was drawn to a list of ideas for future sculptures that I had pinned on the wall. I contemplated each one, hoping to find one that would inspire me so that I could begin working again. But none did. I stayed there for the remainder of the day and the next one without a single inspiration. As nightfall darkened the room, I remembered it was Friday evening and raced to the gallery. I arrived thirty minutes after the preview reception was scheduled to begin. The entry of the gallery was empty, except for the owner, who walked up to me with a newspaper in his hand.

"Congratulations!" he exclaimed sarcastically. "You succeeded in sabotaging your own show."

"What do you mean?" I asked, alarmed.

"Don't tell me you didn't read the review in this morning's paper?" He slapped the newspaper onto my chest, prompting me to take hold of it. As I read the article, he grumbled, "Fortunately, I was able to cancel the catering and ensemble in time."

While reading the article, I exclaimed indignantly, "This is absurd! I can't believe the reporter took such liberties with what I said. I'll ask the editor for a retraction."

"That won't make any difference at this point. Your

patrons won't be returning. That is . . . except for the one who is admiring your new pieces on display in the hall gallery. Perhaps he'll buy all of them." He laughed. "If not, you'll need to clear them out by morning."

As he left, slamming the door behind him, my brother appeared in the entry of the hall gallery. We stood facing one another for a few moments before he said, "Your recent sculptures are extraordinary." His face glowed as he spoke.

"To you alone, it appears."

"Not to you?" he questioned.

"I don't understand them," I said, though I was not accustomed to confiding in him. "It wasn't I who created them."

"That is the creative process," he said, passionate. "That lack of understanding allowed you to experience something that defies the need to be understood and has a power that cannot be controlled or claimed."

Though I had never thought of creativity in the way he described, his words struck me like a lightning bolt. "That power is not mine!" I exclaimed and then questioned, "Or could it be something unique to me?"

Looking into my eyes he said, "Everyone has it, yet most distrust or fear it. To fill that void within themselves, they look for this creative force in others. They mistakenly believe only a few possess it and exalt them, perceiving it as something unique." He smiled broadly. "But for us lucky ones whose creativity goes unnoticed, we do not become distracted from the supernatural experience."

"I could not sculpt solely for my own gratification!" I said, taken aback by his remark.

"Then, who are you creating for?" he asked, challenging my response.

"For others. Their approval validates my work." I paused, realizing the absurdity of my statement, since I had little respect for the opinions and values of my patrons.

For a while I stood motionless before him, pondering our conversation. "Your creative experience is the polar opposite of mine," I said, pensively. "Yours exalts the supernatural experience while mine seems to negate it."

He lowered his head along with his voice. "Next week, my current book will be placed on the bestseller list. Because of the attention it's getting, sales of my other books have soared. When my publisher told me this news yesterday, I felt something sacred to me alone was being taken away. But as we are speaking together just now, I realize creativity is not something that can be taken or given, it simply is. And interfering with it in any way destroys it."

"What then is the reward for our creative efforts?" I asked him.

He looked at me, as the glow returned to his face.

"What's the reward?" I repeated when I heard the Seer say, *Creativity is the omnipotent force that manifests in every action in every being in every moment. It presents itself in countless ways and is experienced as joyful equanimity. Yet that experience goes unnoticed if creativity is desired or averted, claimed or abused.*

After the boy finished speaking, the girl rocked back and forth on the crate, appearing deep in thought.

"Not long after my sister died, I began writing poetry," she confided. "I had never done anything like that before but, for some reason, it came naturally. While composing poems, I felt safe and removed from everything that defined my dreary life. Each poem took several days to complete. When it was finished, I destroyed it, making sure that no one ever read it. I imagined I was ashamed of my poetry, since I had a low opinion of myself. But as you were talking, I realized that wasn't the case at all." Her voice lowered to a whisper. "If I shared my poems with others, I was afraid I would lose that intimacy I had with myself."

"Do you still write poetry?" he asked.

"No," she replied in a melancholy tone. "Once, my father found my notebook and read a poem I had almost finished. In a fit of anger, he tore it up and broke my pencils. I was too afraid to write after that. But sentences still form in poetic meter in my mind." She turned to the boy and said in a whisper, "Thank you." Then she whisked away.

On the day the girl returned, she saw a stout woman talking to the boy. As the woman stood up to leave, the girl overheard her say, "Thank you for lending your ear to this troubled woman, Matau." She handed him a few coins and waddled off.

"Matau," said the girl as she sat down on the crate. "Is that who you are?"

"People call me by different names," he said, "but I don't claim any of them. Matau was her son's name. She told me that he died when he was my age."

"Nothing weighs you down, does it?" she said, laughing. "Not even a name." Excited to share her recent experiences, she began speaking faster. "The other day, I became aware of how preoccupied I am planning every detail of my daily life. I've been living two steps ahead of myself without ever being fully present. On the few occasions that I was able to break this habit, I entered situations with a receptive mind, which was free of preconceptions. I came to realize that useful planning is not belabored, and the best of it seems to be instantaneous and spontaneous." She mused, glancing up at the sky, "Curiously, the times I didn't fall into my planning habit, I felt as if I were getting out of my own way."

"In a sense you were," he said. "You trusted in what you did not know rather than what you thought you did."

"Trusting in what I did not know," she echoed, confirming her experience. "Something else happened to me since I last saw you. The emotions that accompanied the stories circling through my mind were exhausting me. I noticed my breath mirrored those emotions. When I am upset, I tend to hold my breath; when I am frightened, my breath is shallow; when I am critical, it is erratic. Something mysterious led me to fix my attention on the rhythm of my breath, instead of the stories." Her voice rose. "My breath steadied just by watching it, and the stories vanished. I felt blissful, as I do when I watch clouds fancifully floating through the sky."

"That 'something mysterious' was grace," he said.

"Grace?" she questioned. "From where does it come?"

"From nowhere and everywhere. It always is, yet it goes unnoticed when the mind is distracted by thoughts."

"Then everyone is always being blessed," she said, smiling. "I know I certainly am." She took a deep breath before asking him, "What was your next life?"

He sat upright and slowly rotated his shoulders several times before beginning. "This is how it was . . . "

"But Mama, he's not asking for your help," my daughter shouted at me.

My daughter had raised her voice so that I could hear her. The idea of becoming isolated through losing my hearing terrified me. Though my family and friends compassionately raised their voices and slowed their speech whenever they spoke to me, I was aware of their frustration and sensed their relief when our conversations ended.

"I know that," I said, acknowledging her concern. "But while he is at work, he has no one to care for his dying father." Hoping to convince her, I added, "You know as well as I that he never asks anyone for anything."

"Perhaps he has his reasons for not asking," she said, as she leaned toward me and looked into my eyes. "Whenever you get involved in situations like this, you tend to overstep your boundaries."

"That's not so!" I said, annoyed.

Her eyebrows rose. "Do you remember taking in our neighbor's two children when her husband deserted them? You fed those children every day long after the time when she could have cared for them herself."

"But they had become part of our family. I couldn't just send them away," I replied.

"Her son once told me that his mother was a terrible cook and was happy not to have to eat her food. I remember how tired you were during that time. All of us knew she was taking advantage of your kindness and growing less inclined to mother her children."

Though I disagreed with my daughter, I respected her opinion, which wasn't the case when my husband reprimanded me for meddling in the affairs of others. I thought he was being selfish because I wasn't devoting all my attention to him. He often recounted the time I took in a fallen nestling. The parent birds squawked outside of our house day and night. My family begged me to set it free, but I feared that it was too weak to fend for itself. As I was feeding it one morning, it died in my hands. My husband told me that it might have survived had I not been so intent on caring for it.

"You're going to help him, aren't you?" asked my daughter, as though she already knew my answer.

"I have no choice. I can't stand by idle, knowing someone is in need."

Early the next day I went to the man's house before he left for work. When I offered to assist him by making lunch for his bedridden father and staying with him a few hours each afternoon, I sensed his hesitancy. But within moments, his head began nodding, as if involuntarily, and he welcomed my assistance.

When I returned later that morning and introduced myself to the father, I was captivated by his serenity though disturbed by his reservation toward me. My temperament appeared to be opposite from his; I was inclined to engage in conversation with anyone and everyone while he seemed to prefer silence.

In the days that followed, I fed him lunch and spent a few hours at his bedside before leaving. During that time, we exchanged few words as he lay on his back, gazing wide-eyed up at the ceiling. If his body ever moved, it was not detectable to my eyes. On the other hand, I was fidgety, worrying about his comfort and imminent demise. I began wondering if he needed my assistance at all, though I was intent on giving it. On several occasions, I had the uncanny feeling that I was sitting beside him for my benefit rather than his.

As the days passed, I began worrying that my presence was a disturbance to his tranquility. He must have sensed my discomfort and felt compassion for me because, while I was lost in that thought one afternoon, he broke his silence by saying, "You remind me of one of my aunts." I was relieved to hear him speak and surprised that I could clearly hear each of his words. I wondered if my restored sense of hearing was due to his deep voice, unlike my husband's that was a full octave higher and almost indiscernible to my ear.

"Is that so? What do you remember about her?" I asked, curious about how I resembled his aunt.

After pondering my question, he said, "She often told me that I was blessed. But I never understood what she meant because I thought 'blessed' meant to be lucky, and I certainly was not that. A few times I asked her, 'Who is blessing me?' She replied with an enchanted expression on her face, 'It's the eternal Light within you!' Her words were etched into my memory, since she was the only person whom I loved and who loved me while I was growing up."

"What about your parents?" I asked. "Didn't they love you?"

"My father was a gambler. I was told he got caught cheating at cards in a tavern one night and created a ruckus. He got beat up and was rescued by my mother, who was a harlot in the place. They got married just after I was born. But he kept gambling and got killed in another brawl, leaving my mother destitute and unable to care for me."

"Then who took care of you?" I asked, though I hoped I wasn't being too nosey.

"I was shuffled from one place to another throughout my childhood. My mother took me back a few times, but she was so unstable that I never spent more than a couple of months with her. For a few years, I lived with the aunt who reminds me of you, until she died. By the time I was fourteen, I had lived in ten different homes."

"Did *anyone* take kindly to you?"

"Most everyone treated me like an outcast. Without self-respect or proper schooling, I became reckless and attracted trouble wherever I went. When people told me I was unlucky, just like my father, I believed them!"

"Did you finish school?" I asked hesitantly.

"No," he replied, frowning. "I dropped out and took odd jobs to get by. When I was nineteen I helped build a stage in a neighboring town for their harvest festival. I wanted to listen to the local musicians at the festival, so I stayed on after the work was finished. During one of their performances, a girl asked me to dance and, before the evening was over, I asked her to marry me."

"Did you love her?" I asked, imagining this was what changed his life.

"I thought so and she seemed to love me. Shortly after our son was born, I got work on a river barge. By the time I returned home several months later, she had fallen in love with another man and was carrying his child. She ran away with him, leaving me with our son. From then on, my life went downhill. Whatever I attempted to accomplish seemed insurmountable, and I felt defeated even before I began."

"How dreadful!"

"Seemed so at the time. But when I look back at it all, I wouldn't have wanted it any other way," he said with a smile on his face. "If it had been otherwise, I don't imagine I would have experienced 'the turning.'"

"The turning?" I asked, curious as to what he meant. "What brought it about?"

"Grace. It was grace alone," he said, looking intently into my eyes. Then, he looked up at the ceiling and resumed telling me his story. "Like my mother, I could barely take care of my son, much less myself. We moved around, never staying in one place for more than a week at a time.

"Once, my son woke up in the pitch black of night. Disoriented, he asked me, 'Where am I, Papa?' He couldn't have been much more than four years old at the time. I took hold of his pointer finger and pressed it onto his chest. He looked at me questioningly and then fell back to sleep.

"I was still holding my son's finger to his chest when I heard my aunt's voice as clear as day: 'You are blessed by the eternal Light within you.' Her words resonated through me with such urgency and force that I was compelled to look for the Light right then. Thinking that It must be

inside my body, I began searching there. But I quickly realized that who I am could not possibly be found in my body because it functioned independently from the sense I had of myself. *Well then,* I thought. *If I am not in my body, where am I?"*

He abruptly stopped telling me his story when the door flew open, slamming against the wall. Beaming, his son entered the room and told us that he had finished his work early. He seemed pleased to relieve me of my duty. As I prepared to leave, I was touched by the love and respect he showed his father, and the gratitude he expressed to me.

That night, I could not stop thinking about what the father had shared with me. Until then, I never considered I was not my body. Contemplating that notion, I realized that my body managed quite well without my assistance. Yet for some reason, I viewed it as incompetent and, at times, I was even afraid of it. When it inconvenienced me by being out of sorts, I was not inclined to turn to it for guidance. Why would I? I didn't trust it.

I wondered, *How can I have compassion for others when I can't even accept the natural transitions of my own body? I'm always interfering with them.* As I was thinking about this, I imagined I caused my body more harm than good, especially when I dwelled on its failings, like its loss of hearing. In hopes of restoring it, I had taken the advice of others by altering my diet, sleeping with herbs in my ears and putting drops of medicinal oil in them every morning. None of these remedies seemed to help, as my hearing was getting worse. Yet I feared that if I were to discontinue any of them I might lose my hearing altogether. So I held onto my fears ever more tightly.

The next day, I anticipated the father would continue telling me about his experience after I fed him lunch. But he remained silent, staring at the ceiling. Just before the time I usually left, I built up enough courage to ask him if he would continue his story. He appeared confused by my request, as if he had forgotten our conversation of the previous day.

"You realized you were not your body," I reminded him.

"Oh yes!" he exclaimed and continued his story where he had left off. "I was certain that I was not to be found in my body. *Then I must be in my mind,* I thought, since it had always given me the impression that it was the commander of my body. *But how could I be found there? My mind is unreliable and often leads me astray.* Looking at my mind straight on, I realized it is just a jumble of thoughts."

With a whimsical look in his eyes, he stared at me squarely and asked, "How can I be found in a mind that is not trustable?" A smile crept over his face, and he resumed gazing at the ceiling without saying another word. Shortly after that, I left.

That evening, I found myself observing my thoughts. I had always trusted them implicitly, believing them to be true and following them wherever they went. But while scrutinizing their nature, I could see that they were the cause of my anxieties. *Am I a helpless victim to their chaotic ramblings?* I wondered. All this thinking led me to the question that the father had left with me: If I am not to be found in my body or my mind, then where am I?

After serving him lunch the next day, I asked him straightaway, "The turning that you spoke of, what was the turning?"

"Oh yes, the turning!" he exclaimed and then continued his story. "I had closed my eyes, ever so tightly, and asked myself, *Who am I?* I kept repeating the question in hopes of finding the answer. Then, in a split second, all the energy I was exerting left me. My body felt like it had melted away, and my thoughts scattered into space. When my eyes opened, beams of light projected from my eyes." He paused with an uncertain expression on his face. "Quite honestly, I couldn't tell you if they were coming from outside or inside of me. Within the beam projecting from my left eye, images appeared of my physical body in constant transformation, from infancy to adulthood and back again. Within the beam from my right eye, images appeared of all the different characters I had ever imagined myself to be. I noticed that the two sets of images influenced each other though they were not connected in any way. Surrounding these beams of light were images of things I perceived as the world. While viewing this grand spectacle, I realized that what I was seeking could not be found in anything I was seeing, but rather in the one who was seeing it all."

He turned to me, as though checking to see if I was still following him. When I nodded, he continued, "I found the eternal Light that my aunt had seen within me. Yet it was not only inside me but everywhere! Light was all there was." His attention drifted away from her. "Light is who I am—unruffled and unrufflable awareness that is not limited by a single thought. I received this insight with such clarity that I could not possibly doubt it."

He paused, having come to the end of his story. "This happened well over a half century ago. Since then, nothing has presented itself as a problem to me, and the anxiety that once paralyzed me never showed its face again." He looked wistfully at me and then turned his attention to the ceiling.

Sitting at his bedside each day thereafter, I was captivated by his radiance. From time to time, I even imagined I was experiencing the Light of consciousness, as he had described. During that time my fears were dispelled, one by one.

One day while I was sitting beside him, his eyes closed ever so slowly, never to open again. His passage coincided with my complete loss of hearing. The only words I heard after that were from the Seer, who said,

*To surrender superfluous thoughts, one after the next,
again and again, is to abide in that which has no limits or
definitions. Within that formless equanimity of indescribable
majesty, one discovers oneself to be all that cannot be known.*

"I am awareness," the girl said, reiterating the father's
words. "When he said that, I reflected on the habit of my mind—
always reaching for the next word, the next idea, the next activity—and how that habit keeps me from being awareness." The
smile on her face faded. "I have been looking outside of myself
to find the truth, which actually turns me away from it as you
have often told me. Yet my social conditioning, along with
everything I have been taught, encourages me to look outside of
myself." She paused, looking up at the sky. "I imagine to reverse
that movement would be like trying to swim upstream while
floating downstream in a strong current." Her eyes glazed over
with tears. "What will it take for me to turn?"

"Patience, and surrendering the false sense that you can
control the inevitable," he said softly.

She stared at him, trembling. Within moments, her posture
relaxed and a tear fell from her dry eyes. She touched his hands
and walked away.

The next day, the boy was sitting by himself in the hot sun
when the beggars began laughing a short distance from him.
Amid their frivolity, the girl's familiar laugh resounded above
the others. When she sat down beside him, he asked, "What gave
them such pleasure?"

"Apples," she said.

She parted his hands and placed an apple between them. He
grinned and began eating it.

"The Light," the girl said in a tone of urgency. "The father
spoke of It as if It could always be seen. So I have been sitting
with my eyes closed for long periods of time looking for It. I
am accustomed to see only darkness with my eyes closed, yet,
several times, I had a clear sense of the Light. However, when I
opened my eyes, It instantly disappeared."

She watched the boy eating the apple for a while before continuing. "While the father was looking at the ceiling, he saw the Light with his eyes wide open. So I imagined I could see It with my eyes open as well. When I attempted to do this, my attention was taken by whatever appeared before them. From what you have shared with me, I sense the Light is always present. But I cannot see It because my attention gets distracted by things outside of me."

The boy set the apple down on his lap and said, "Watching actors on stage, you become absorbed in their performances and readily identify with them, losing sight of who you are." He picked up the apple as though he were about to begin eating. But instead, he set it down again and continued, "Who you imagine yourself to be is a notion composed of many aspects, including your physical features, intellectual abilities, habits, beliefs, achievements, preferences and perceptions. This ever-changing notion is constantly making appearances and then leaving, like actors on stage. But in its absence, something remains that never changes. That something sees and knows everything that can be known but is without aspects and is not governed by the intellect. You are that alone, while the illusive actors that you imagine yourself to be have been taking the limelight, along with all the accolades."

"Taking all the accolades while making my life miserable," she said blithely. "I imagine it is not necessary to find the Light, since It is always within me. And, it is not necessary to rid myself of the actors or change them in any way, since they are just passing phenomena, like clouds in the sky." She looked at the boy and said with earnestness, "I need to place my trust in what I do not know rather than what I think I know."

She began rocking back and forth on the crate while muttering to herself. "I had always assumed my mind was behind my physical senses. But I'm now seeing that it is only the interpreter of them and actually obscures the clarity of awareness, which alone is behind my senses." She frowned, appearing mystified by her train of thoughts. "Awareness must also be the one behind the voice in my head."

After the boy finished eating the apple, she asked him to tell her his next past life. Tossing the core into his mouth, he swallowed it and then began, "This is how it was . . . "

"I see that your son has mastered the skills he's learned from his warrior training," said the tribal chief, commending me. "He has now reached the age at which he will need to choose his life vocation."

From the ages of six to sixteen, boys received an education in each tribal skill. During their seventeenth year, they were required to choose one as their livelihood at the annual summer solstice ceremony.

"He was born to be a warrior," I said. "His wit, strength and agility far exceed those of his peers."

"I know you are proud of your son and would like him to follow in your footsteps. But do you think that will be his choice?" questioned the chief.

"I'm beginning to have doubts," I replied with a sigh. "While growing up, he always turned to me for guidance. But nowadays when we speak about his life ambition, he seems to have lost interest in becoming a warrior and ignores my suggestions."

"You might consider visiting the wisdom elder. He can counsel you in this matter."

Later that afternoon my son ran up to me with a drum tucked under his arm. Grinning, he said, "The drummer elder told me that if I practice with the drummers every day, I can perform with them during the ceremony of the one-eyed crow."

"Oh? Is that so?" I said with a tone of indifference, since I did not want to encourage his aspiration. My response upset him, as evidenced by his indignation. When we parted, I went to the wisdom elder.

"I want my son to be a warrior," I stated after he invited me into his hut. "I have coached him at each level of warrior training and know his strengths and weaknesses better than he does. While growing up, he sought my guidance. But now he shuns it, though he seems unable to make a decision on his own. He is versatile and has many interests. At one time, he wanted to be a hunter and, at other times, an artisan and practitioner."

After relating the encounter I just had with my son, I said, "I know he has an interest in drumming, but he does not have a good sense of rhythm. So I discourage him from pursuing that vocation."

"I do not doubt what you say," said the elder. "However, you are perceiving your son as an extension of yourself, which prevents you from seeing who he is. Your tendency to have him be as you saw him in the past and as you hope he will be in the future keeps you from seeing his truth, which stands between the past and the future."

Though I found little consolation in his response, I asked him what he would recommend that I do.

"Nothing," he replied. "If you just remain present, you will not mistake your thoughts as the ultimate reality. And if he should request your counsel, offer it by teaching him how to answer his own questions."

"He is young and prone to make mistakes," I said. "If I withhold my guidance at this turning point in his life, I will never forgive myself."

"You have come to me for counsel," replied the elder curtly. "However, you are not obliged to take it."

In the days that followed, my son avoided me. When we were together, I didn't initiate conversation with him. In his absence, I found myself plotting ways to influence his decision and rehearsed conversations that would persuade him to follow my wishes. I feared that if I gave him my advice outright, he would become upset. So instead, I decided to ask him questions that would sway his decision, and he would choose to become a warrior.

When I saw my son the day before the solstice, he said he was still undecided about his vocation.

"On what are you basing your decision?" I asked.

"My lifework must be fulfilling and enable me to pursue my ambitions," he replied.

"What are your ambitions?"

He pondered my question and then said candidly, "To raise the standard of my chosen vocation, mentor those who follow me and become a respected elder of the community."

"Noble aspirations, indeed," I said. "Do you know your talents?"

"My talents are not my primary concern in making this decision because they change. While I was growing up, I could throw a spear farther than any of my peers. Now, many of them surpass my ability."

"That is because you have not developed your skills in earnest!" I blurted, losing my composure. "Instead, you divert your energies in many directions. You are most suited to be a warrior, the most respected vocation of our tribe. If you improve your skills, you will attain a high ranking among your peers. Then you will be given a position of leadership, which will later earn you a seat beside me on the chief's council." My voice rose as if he were standing a distance from me. "By doing this, you would serve your community best!"

"This is *my* decision, not yours," he shouted and stomped off.

Regretting my outburst, I returned to the wisdom elder and told him what had just transpired between my son and me.

"My tongue got away from me," I said. "I could not stop myself from advising him."

"Your tongue was not the problem. It is your headstrong desire," he replied.

"What you say is true. The moment my son left I realized that I'm not willing to let him go. I have believed that if he follows my guidance, he will continue to turn to me as his father."

"But at his age you can no longer father him," he said. "He has become a man, your fellow tribesman."

"Yes. I know that, but a part of me refuses to accept it," I responded, overcome with a sudden feeling of remorse. "If only I could make amends for my ignorance."

"What!" exclaimed the elder. "Have you forgotten the purpose of the 'sitting' that precedes the vocation ceremony tomorrow? The rite enables fathers to give their sons the independence they require to become men."

"At this point, an apology would appear dishonest," I said, "or, worse yet, manipulative."

"I am not suggesting you apologize. Just sit directly in front of him and look into his eyes without saying a word or following after a single thought that enters your mind."

"What purpose would that serve?" I questioned.

The wisdom elder leaned toward me and looked deeply into my eyes. As I held his gaze, I was unable to follow my thoughts. Instead, my emptied mind was filled with an omniscient awareness that saw beyond my illusions. As though a cloud of smoke blocking my vision had suddenly dissipated, I was freed from the perceptions and beliefs that obstructed my understanding.

"In this moment, does anything separate you from me?" he asked.

"Nothing," I replied, confounded. "Nothing separates us."

"This is how it is for you and your son," he said. "Nothing separates you, except your thoughts."

"But how can I return here tomorrow evening while sitting with my son?" I asked. "I mean . . . in this place where I am right now?"

"Return?" he laughed. "You answer your own question. You are here right now just as you will be tomorrow while sitting with your son. Trust in what you do not know, and all will be well."

As the students began joining their fathers for the

sitting the next evening, I spotted my son in the distance. He appeared reluctant to approach me. When he sat down a short distance from me, I repositioned myself directly in front of him and looked into his eyes. He fidgeted and seemed intent on pulling away from my gaze. As his eyes darted back and forth between mine, I began to doubt my ability to trust in all that I did not know.

"Do you have anything to tell me?" he asked with a quiver in his voice.

I wanted to say 'no' but nothing came out of my mouth. I held my gaze, though his apparent discomfort challenged my confidence. In time, his posture eased and I experienced the unifying omniscience as I had the previous day. I sensed he was also experiencing it when his eyes steadied and his body suddenly relaxed.

The chief sounded his horn to summon the students and their fathers. My son and I were so absorbed in our reunion that we were the last to stand up and join the assembly. The ceremonial fire was lit in conjunction with a series of rituals. Then a group of warriors formed a line and began dancing and chanting as they circled the fire. While watching the spectacle, I felt my son lean into my side, which

confirmed to me that nothing stood between us—neither a thought nor an emotion.

As the moon began its ascent in the heavens, the chief sounded his horn again, and the seven vocational elders took their places behind him. He nodded to the artisan elder to call the students who had chosen that vocation. A group of students stepped forward and circled the fire three times before standing behind their elder.

Next, the drummer elder called out for the students who had chosen to follow his lead. My son stepped forward with that group. He turned to me before joining his peers, who had already begun circling the fire. I nodded, confirming his decision, though my heart sank. In my disappointment, a sea of thoughts separated me from him once again. I felt as though I had lost not only my son but myself as well. I questioned myself, *Who am I without him?* But I could not find the answer.

The warrior elder was last to call his students. As the remaining students stepped forward and began circling the fire, I was surprised to see my son joining them. After they assembled beside the warrior elder, the chief signaled for my son to stand beside him.

"This student requested two vocations," announced the chief. "And because he has exceptional skills in both of them, the warrior elder has given his consent for him to perform with the drummers at all of our sacred ceremonies."

The light of the ceremonial fire began fading as I heard the Seer say,

Wisdom is self-knowledge, which is awareness of awareness, or consciousness. Consciousness is existence, which is simply being, or unwavering joy. Unwavering joy has no form, color or attributes and is free of concepts or thoughts. Wisdom is not found in thoughts but in the space between them.

Listening to the boy tell his past life, the girl was enthralled and barely moved. But the moment he stopped, her whole being enlivened.

"Attempting to control your circumstances kept you from happiness in that life," she said, forthright, "as it has for me. When you first began conveying your past lives, I couldn't imagine quieting my mind. But I soon discovered that I could actually let go of my thoughts." She paused, looking down at the ground. "That is except for the one that is central to all of them: the 'I' thought. The times I do let go of it, no other thoughts arise, and my mind is peaceful. Yet I am resistant to let it go because the 'I' thought is familiar to me and without it, I feel helpless." She smiled and shrugged her shoulders. "Even though I am fully aware that this central thought is demanding, critical and allows few liberties, I have always considered it to be my friend." Her voice rose. "And in friendship, one accepts the good along with the bad. Isn't that so?"

"One must always be true to oneself," he said calmly. "Not to the idea of who one imagines oneself to be."

She nodded. "I understand what you say, but without the 'I' thought, I fear I could no longer control the events of my life." She laughed. "As though I ever could. What ties me to such a belief?"

"As you have just said—fear," he replied. "Fear of losing the one who you imagine yourself to be."

"Yes!" she exclaimed after pondering his response. "I am definitely afraid of losing that. What does it take to overcome fear?"

"Humility, which is the willingness to let go. This is your true nature."

"I am not a particularly humble person," she mused.

For a while they sat in silence. Then she touched the boy's hand affectionately and walked away.

When the girl sat down beside him the next day, she appeared fidgety. "I feel like I have been asking you the same questions, over and over again, and you have been giving me the same answers. I thought I understood what you have been telling me, but only now am I beginning to understand. How is this?"

He turned toward her and said, "Initially, you were listening with your ears, trying to gain understanding through your mind. Now you are listening with your heart, which already knows the truth."

From her intonations, she appeared to understand his explanation. "I believed happiness was something found outside of me. But your past lives have shown me that it isn't apart from me; only my mind keeps me from it."

She took a deep breath before asking him to tell her his next past life. Before she exhaled, he nodded and said, "This is how it was . . ."

"I will be waiting for you in front of the school building when you are dismissed today," my mother said to me. "Your aunt is not able to come anymore. Instead of going to her home, you will stay with me while I look after the old woman I tend to." I was eleven years old and the eldest of my classmates by at least two years, not because I was stupid but because I had missed several years of schooling.

"Yes, mother," I replied obediently.

When I left school with the other students that day, I saw my mother waving her hand and shouting, "Over here!" I stood beside her as she rummaged through her handbag and pulled out a hat.

"Here," she said. "Put this on." Without my assistance, she placed the hat on my head and pulled its wide brim down over my face.

After arranging the hat to her satisfaction, she took hold of my hand and led me through the backstreets where few people walked. Each time we came upon a passerby, she quickened her pace because she was ashamed of my appearance.

My aunt had told me that my disfigured face was a hardship for my mother. She also told me that when my father first looked at me, just after I was born, he ran away and was never seen again. My mother often blamed me for being the cause of her misfortunes, yet I found no reason to fault her for that. In my heart, I knew she loved me, even though she never expressed these sentiments.

When people questioned my mother about my deformity, she would become nervous and acted as if it were her own. Although my appearance seemed to define her life, it was of little consequence to me. Strangers distorted their faces upon seeing me, but I assumed it was simply their manner. At school, I was the subject of constant ridicule among my classmates, who took every opportunity to distance themselves from me. On the other hand, their behavior gave rise to a profound sense of compassion for them within me, which brought me as close to them as I was to myself. I realized their fears were unfounded and that, in reality, nothing stood between us.

"What are you doing in bed at this time?" yelled my mother as we entered the home of the old woman. The prevailing color of the single-room apartment was grey; even the light that emanated from the lamp had a grey

tinge to it. "If you don't get up, you'll get bedsores again. And you know how miserable that makes you."

"I'm tired of getting up, " she said, disgruntled. "I just want to sleep forever."

"Stop that nonsense!" scoffed my mother.

"Nonsense, you say? How would you like to discover another part of your body was failing every time you tried to get out of bed? You too would be afraid to open your eyes in the morning."

My mother ignored her response and introduced me. "This is my son. He will be staying here while I tend to you in the afternoons." She took off my hat. But before she could hide my face from view, which was her habit, the woman shrieked, "What's wrong with him?"

"Nothing!" exclaimed my mother. "There is *nothing* wrong with him."

"Are you telling me the truth? He doesn't have a disease or something contagious, does he?" Nervously fiddling with the top button of her blouse, the old woman blurted out, "He has the ugliest face I have ever seen."

"You're one to talk," snapped my mother. "Can you not see your own face in the mirror?"

"I'll have you know I was considered the most beautiful dancer that ever performed at the Royal Theater!" She stared into space while continuing, "One night, the crown prince himself came backstage and told me that I—"

My mother interrupted her, saying, "You've told this story so many times I might believe it to be true, if it didn't change with each telling. Go on! Get yourself out of bed and sit in your chair or you won't be eating today." Then she led me to the table and told me to do my studies.

The old woman slithered out of bed with her attention fixed on me, as though I were a dangerous animal. Watching her creep across the room, I saw that her stooped posture made her even shorter than I. She sat down directly across from me and continued to stare. When I stared back, I was again filled with an awe-inspiring sense of compassion.

"If you dribble your food down the front of your blouse today, I won't change it," threatened my mother.

"What! Do you think I enjoy soiling my clothes?" yelled the old woman.

I had never heard my mother speak so harshly. At first I felt concern for the old woman. But as I listened to the two women argue, I sensed they were finding more pleasure in their confrontation than displeasure.

Each day that followed was similar to the last; the two women bickered while I did my studies. After my mother served the meal, she cleaned the house. Then she sat on the other side of the room beside the window and began knitting until she fell asleep. Some days, she left us for a while to do the shopping or wash clothes down the street.

The old woman remained in her chair all afternoon and continued to stare at me while I studied. Yet with each passing day, I noticed she was growing less frightened of me. After my mother fell asleep one afternoon, I asked the old woman if she would tell me about the Royal Theater.

"Why would that be of interest to you?" she asked curtly.

"I'm reading about its history," I replied, holding up my book.

"Is that so?" she said, appearing curious. "Will you read it to me?"

I nodded and began reading about how the theater was built and why it was destroyed during the battle that united the northern and southern provinces.

When I finished, she said, "I wonder why the account doesn't mention the extraordinary people who performed on its stage."

"Would you tell me about them?" I asked with interest.

She looked at me with a radiant smile that transformed her face and offered me a glimpse of how she might have looked as a young woman. That day, she recounted a story about one of the people with whom she performed at the Royal Theater, and each afternoon after my mother fell asleep, she told me about another. When she finished, she would ask me to read my daily lesson.

After I read to her one day, she said candidly, "You have a marvelous voice. Only the most learned actors have the ability to enunciate and resonate their voices as well as you." She stared at me as if waiting for my response. But since I remained silent, she continued, "When I was your age, I played with my friends in the field, which is now the park you can see from my window. Do you ever go there to play?"

"No," I replied.

"Why not? Don't you have any friends?" she asked.

I shook my head.

She stared at me, appearing troubled by my response. After a few moments, she mumbled, "May I be your friend?"

I nodded and asked, "Can we go to the park?"

Taken aback by my request, she exclaimed, "I can't go there! I haven't left this room in over fifteen years."

"Why not?" I asked.

She frowned and hesitantly replied, "Well, because someone might recognize me and see that I have become a decrepit old woman. Their memory of the beautiful young dancer who performed at the Royal Theater would be lost forever."

"Memory?" I asked. "You are still beautiful."

Amused by my comment, she began laughing so loud that my mother woke up.

"What's going on over there?" asked my mother as she hurried to the table and looked me straight in the eye. "Is she making fun of you again?"

"No," I said. "She's just happy."

"Happy!" she exclaimed. "You must mean crazy."

"Perhaps I am crazy," sneered the old woman. "But no more than you."

When my mother left to do the shopping the next afternoon, the old woman said, "I've been a hypocrite, offering you my friendship and then withholding it. The real reason I won't take you to the park is that I don't like people staring at me. When I was onstage, their stares brought me much happiness. Now, they make me feel alone and ashamed of the way I look." She lowered her head.

"You wouldn't have to worry about that if we were together," I said. "People usually look away when they see me."

She didn't respond. Instead, she told me another story about one of the performers of the Royal Theater. As our friendship developed, her morose disposition turned around. She was even cheerful and often cooperated with my mother.

One afternoon after my mother left with the clothes that needed washing, the old woman opened her armoire and took out an overcoat. "You'll have to help me put on my shoes," she said as she went to the window and looked down at the park.

"Where are you going?" I asked.

"*We* are going to the park," she replied with a glint in her eyes.

"But we need to tell my mother," I said, disturbed.

"She wouldn't allow it. Don't worry. We'll be back well before she returns," she assured me. "Now help me on with my shoes!"

Before we descended the stairway, she said, "Take a firm hold of my arm so I don't fall." On the way to the park, she often stopped to catch her breath. In those moments, she would glance up at the sky with an ecstatic smile on her face. When we got there, several people were waiting in line to use the swings, so we walked to the empty bench beside them. But before we sat down, everyone left. I looked at the swings longingly.

"Go ahead," she said, insistent. "I'll sit here and watch you." As I was swinging back and forth in front of her, her head followed my glide. I imagined she was enjoying the sensation as much as I.

On our way back to her home, she stopped and looked at me with a troubled expression on her face. "The older I get, the smaller my world becomes," she confided. "It has become so small, in fact, that it doesn't extend beyond my body. As I was watching you swing, all the limitations that made my world small disappeared completely." She mumbled to herself as she continued walking. "Where did they go? Could I have only imagined them?"

We returned to the grey room long before my mother. Since she was unsuspecting of our escapade, we made a habit of going to the park every time she went out.

While at the park one afternoon, I pointed to the seesaw and asked, "Can we do that together?"

Her eyes opened wide as if my very question was frightening. "I'd fall off if you weren't always by my side."

"I'll stay beside you," I promised her.

She gave me her hand reluctantly, and I led her to the seesaw. Once she sat down on the plank and took hold of the handlebar in front of her, she seemed to gain confidence. I stood beside her, slowly raising and lowering the plank until her anxieties were relieved. Then I sat down on the opposite side of the plank, and we began teetering up and down. Each time she was lifted into the air, she made childlike sounds of delight. In her amusement, she lost track of time until I reminded her it was getting late. On the way back to her home that afternoon, she didn't pause to rest. When we opened the door to the grey room, my mother met us with a stern expression on her face. Looking at her, I was filled with remorse for having deceived her.

"Where have you been?" she asked in an angry tone.

"At the park," the old woman said with a broadening smile.

Annoyed by her response, my mother stood staring at us. Then she released a deep sigh and said to me, "Go do your homework."

"Will you come with us next time?" I asked.

She shook her head and said, "There won't be a next time."

"Why not?" questioned the old woman, taunting her. "Tell him you'll come with us. You have no cause to be ashamed of him. If anything gives you cause for shame, it should be your attitude toward him. Shame on *you*!"

As she spoke, my mother turned pale and cowered. I could not bear to see the one I loved being persecuted, but I did not know how to defend her. The old woman continued using me to substantiate her accusations, which separated me from my mother. I had never known vengeance but, in that moment, it was all I knew.

"Your son's brilliance far outshines that of anyone I've ever known," said the old woman, continuing to chastise my mother. "And you've kept him locked away as though he were—"

Her tirade abruptly ended when I uttered a loathsome, guttural cry that could be heard far beyond the confines of the grey room. The countenance of the old woman turned as grey as ash, and a violent tremor overtook my body. My mother grabbed hold of me and held me tight in her arms, as she had never done before. The room darkened as the Seer said,

Thoughts are the cause of limitations. Limitations form the boundaries of the mind. Without limitations, the mind is boundless.

When the boy finished speaking, the girl asked, "Vengeance was your limitation, wasn't it?" Without waiting for his response, she continued. "You couldn't let go of it, even though it was painful. Certainly, your reaction was natural and justifiable. Yet by holding onto your vengeance, you were held in its bondage. Isn't that so?"

His hand extended to a passerby. When it returned to his lap, he nodded.

"In each of your past lives, your inability to let go of your limitation was the cause of your suffering," she said. "Was it also the reason you kept returning to live one life after the next?"

Again he nodded.

"At one time, I questioned your words," she continued. "Now I hear them, even in the silent space between us."

She fidgeted as she rocked back and forth. "I have never fallen in love," she said shyly, "but I imagine what I am experiencing in this very moment is similar to that."

"It is that," he affirmed. "Love is your nature. You are experiencing your very nature."

Her breath quickened as she said, "I do not doubt what you say. But I only find you in that space."

Flustered, she hurried away without touching his hand.

The next morning, the beggars hurriedly formed a single row on both sides of the blind boy when they heard the sounds of an approaching funeral procession. During these events, it was customary for relatives of the deceased to give alms to the poor, as the offerings were believed to free the transitioning souls from the throes of the material world.

Several spry young men led the procession. They carried tall baskets filled with flower petals and strewed them into the air as they walked. Minstrels with horns, drums and stringed instruments followed them, playing the lively yet reverent melodies that were reserved for such occasions. Following the minstrels, four stout men carried an open litter on their shoulders upon which the deceased man was securely fastened in a seated position. He had been blindfolded so the trappings of the visual world would not tempt him to remain as an aimless ghost. Throngs of relatives and friends trailed after the litter through the streets.

As the procession passed before the mendicants, several relatives handed out coins. From amid the crowd, a dark shadow fell over the young beggar. A tall stranger had planted himself directly in front of him. Within moments, the stranger fell to his knees and placed his hands on the young beggar's head. The stranger's fingers cascaded down the young beggar's face like water, touching every curve and crevice along the way.

"This is my brother Ahnu," said the girl as she knelt beside the boy. She paused for a few moments before explaining her brother's behavior. "He has wanted to meet you ever since I told him about our first encounter. Each time I return home after talking to you, he pleads for me to tell him everything you said. Perhaps it is his enthusiasm that enables me to recount your words and past lives in such detail. Curiously, he somehow knows if I omit something and insists that I remember it before continuing."

Her voice softened as she looked at her brother. "Every day since we were children, I have read to him and taught him everything I had learned in school. I've been his teacher, even though he is far more intelligent than I," she said, smiling. "He would often ask me questions about the things I taught him but, beyond that, we never spoke. He lived in a different world. However, since you came into our lives, we have become brother and sister as though for the first time."

The boy sat motionless while Ahnu groped his head, neck, shoulders, arms and each of his fingers. Then Ahnu held the boy's hands, as though they were sacred, and placed them on his head. "Now, you see me," he requested meekly.

"I can already see you," replied the boy amiably and pulled his hands away.

"Yes. Ram sees without eyes because Ram is the Seer."

"Ram?" the boy questioned.

The girl explained, "Ram was the first word he ever spoke. It was also the name of his best and only friend, who never leaves his side."

The boy nodded in understanding but remained silent for a

long while. Then he placed his hand on Ahnu's shoulder and said decisively, "I am Ram."

An ecstatic smile swept across Ahnu's face and his posture lifted. Appearing alarmed, Ram redirected his attention toward the girl and asked, "Why are you crying?"

"How is it you see only my tears and not his?" she questioned, smiling. "Mine come from joy in seeing those in my brother's eyes. Until this moment, he has not shown such emotion."

Ahnu leaned a few inches from Ram. "That is because I have only known darkness," he said. "I come to you as a beggar, hoping you will give me Light."

"How can I give you something you already have?" asked Ram.

Ahnu frowned and said, "We were both born blind, yet you see Light and I don't. How is this?"

"You were born of Light, just as I was. You have simply lost sight of It."

Ahnu remained silent for a few moments before saying, "I understand everything you have told my sister. But still I cannot see Light. Whenever I become discouraged and upset with myself, my sister reminds me to let go of my thoughts. When I attempt to do so, I lose what is safe and familiar to me. I lose Ram, my only friend in the frightening world in which I am trapped."

"Why is it frightening to you?"

"Because I don't understand it."

"The world in which you believe you are trapped does not exist, in that it is ever changing like your imaginary friend. You have no reason to fear it but every reason to let go of your belief."

Ahnu appeared mesmerized as he was listening. When the girl told her brother that it was time for them to leave, he did not respond. So she took hold of his hand and led him away after touching Ram's hand.

When the girl returned with her brother the next day, Ram was nowhere to be seen. Appearing like lost children, the two siblings milled around the area where he usually begged.

"Where can he be?" asked Ahnu anxiously.

"He'll be here," replied his sister with assurance. "I usually come later than this."

She stretched her neck, looking down the road to see if he was coming. "Listen! I think I hear the group of them laughing in the distance." As the beggars rounded the corner, she shouted, excited, "There's Ram! He's walking alongside the others." She stood on a curb to get a better look. "They are a motley group, erratic and clumsy in their procession. That is, except for Ram. His stride is steady and smooth. He appears to be alone among them, not part of their frivolity."

When the group stopped to set up their makeshift camp for the day, Ram continued walking until he came directly before the siblings.

"I have never seen you standing," said the girl shyly. "You are much taller than I imagined."

"I stand exactly between the two of you," he said with a jaunty smile. "You are the shortest and your brother the tallest." He then sat down at their feet.

The girl fetched a crate and set it beside him while her brother immediately sat on the ground in front of him. Enthusiastically, the siblings began speaking at the same time. "You move about as if you have sight," said the girl while her brother asked, "How can you walk without assistance?"

"I can see, though not with my eyes. When I walk, I am aware of the things around me. They come to me, rather than I to them, and identify themselves in such a way that my body knows how to move in relation to them."

The two listened with their mouths agape.

"You must have a sixth sense," declared Ahnu, squirming as he was not accustomed to sitting cross-legged.

"We all have a sixth sense," replied Ram. "Though few use it."

The girl chimed in, "Yesterday, you told my brother that you already knew what he looked like. If this is so, you must know the appearance of everyone."

"I do," replied Ram. "But not in the way you imagine. I receive an impression of people by the Light they emit and the colors that surround them."

"But you told me . . . you said," stammered Ahnu, "you said you could see me. But I have no Light."

"You do. Though you are not seeing It, I am."

"I want nothing more than to see Light as you do," said Ahnu fervently. "My life is meaningless as it is."

"If your yearning is true, it will be so," stated Ram. "That is certain."

"These are the very words you said to me when we first met!" exclaimed the girl. She turned toward her brother and whispered, "Trust what he says."

Ahnu shrugged his shoulders and said to Ram, "I don't doubt what you say nor do I doubt my sincerity. What I doubt is my ability. I have never done anything for myself."

For a long while, the three sat together without speaking.

"The colors you see. What do they signify?" asked Ahnu.

"Nothing that can be explained. Each has a unique quality, and when they blend together, they reveal other qualities. Altogether, they form a language that is transmitted faster than thought."

Ahnu continued to ask Ram questions while his sister sat on the crate with her eyes closed. After awhile, she opened her eyes and said, "We must go now." She touched Ram's hand before leading her brother away.

Without fail, the girl returned with her brother each day thereafter. She would sit on the crate beside Ram and close her eyes, while her brother sat in front of him and asked him question after question.

"When I seek myself, I do not like who I find. So I turn away. What am I to do?" asked Ahnu, downhearted.

Ram remained silent. After a while Ahnu rephrased his question. "I hate who I believe myself to be. No matter how hard I try, I cannot let go of those feelings. Is there no hope for me?"

Ram remained silent.

"Why won't you answer me?" asked Ahnu, frustrated.

His sister's eyes sprung open. "He has been answering your questions!" she scolded. "Have you not been listening?"

"I . . . I was," stammered Ahnu, confused by her accusation.

Equally as puzzled, she skewed her head and looked at Ram. "You did answer him . . . didn't you?" Without waiting for his response, she muttered to herself, "Could I have heard words that were not spoken?"

As the days passed, Ahnu had fewer questions. Sometimes Ram answered them directly and other times not. After a while, Ahnu would become quiet and reposition himself beside Ram. As passersby approached the three sitting in a row, Ram was the only one who greeted them by reaching out his open hand.

After a while, the girl said to her brother, "We must go now."

"You go without me, Carma. I want to stay."

"Carma?" Ram questioned. "Is this your name?"

"My full name is Carismeika, but most people call me the shortened form," she replied. Then she turned to her brother and spoke curtly. "You can't stay here. How can you manage by yourself? You don't want to impose on Ram by having him look after you, do you?"

"I won't go!" said Ahnu adamantly. "And I won't be a burden to him. I'll remain here in this very place until the Light comes."

Carma raised her voice. "Imagine how it would be for me to go home without you! Mama would become hysterical and our father furious with me. If you remain, I will have to stay here as well." She relaxed her tone and said, "Ram has told you that the Light is already within you. Trust him."

Acquiescing to his sister, Ahnu dropped his head and extended his hand. In silence, the two walked away.

The next morning, the townspeople began mingling in the streets before dawn, as it was the day of their spring festival. Being in a festive mood, they were unusually friendly toward one another and generous to those in need.

The beggars looked forward to this occasion as a day of

plenty. They assembled themselves in a row, ready to perform for the townsmen by playing the part of downtrodden unfortunates worthy of alms. Ram sat among them, though his demeanor hadn't changed from the day before.

As the morning progressed, people filled the streets in growing numbers. Scurrying about, they occasionally dropped coins in the outstretched hands of the beggars who, like magicians, artfully concealed the gifts in the folds of their clothing so their hands would always appear empty and in need.

When Carma and her brother arrived that afternoon, the streets were so crowded that they were unable to get close to Ram.

"I can barely see him," she said to her brother. "He is surrounded by people giving him coins, food . . . even clothing. We'd best leave and come back tomorrow."

"No, Carma. Please," pleaded her brother. "Can we not just stand near him for a short while?"

She conceded to his wish and the two plodded their way through the crowd. When they could go no further she stopped, squeezed her brother's hand and closed her eyes.

Meanwhile, a woman had sat on the ground beside Ram and was frantically trying to put a pair of shoes on him that were too small for his feet. Another woman was putting food on a plate that she had placed in his hands.

After the two women left, Ram turned toward Carma and her brother. "Come!" he called out. "Take this food. It is more than I can manage."

Immediately, the two made their way to him and knelt by his side.

"How did you know we were standing behind you amid all this commotion?" asked Carma, surprised.

With a whimsical smile, he replied, "Could I have heard your words if they were not spoken?"

Hordes of people jostled the three from one place to another, while the volume of nearby music increased and took every surrounding sound with it. Carma touched Ram's hand and disappeared into the masses with her brother.

When the two returned the next day, neither Ram nor any of the beggars were in sight. Forlorn, they stood holding hands in the place where they usually found him. After a time, they sat down—Carma on the crate and Ahnu on the ground beside her. They remained for a longer time than usual before giving up hope and solemnly walking home.

Steadfast, they returned the next day and the day after that. As they waited, sitting side by side, occasional passersby placed coins in Ahnu's lap.

"Has he disappeared?" he asked his sister. "Or was he just a figment of our imaginations?"

She shook her head and said, "He's at the mercy of the other beggars and goes where they go." She took hold of his hand and led him across the street.

Approaching the fruit vendor, she asked, "Have you seen the beggars recently?"

The vendor looked at her with a broadening grin. "I don't expect to see them for a while, perhaps for weeks or even months to come. With their pockets full of coins, I imagine they are somewhere feasting and celebrating their good fortune."

"Where might that be?" she asked, hopeful.

"I don't rightly know, miss. But I reckon somewhere at the end of this road near the river," he replied, pointing nonchalantly off into the distance.

Carma nodded to the vendor and proceeded down the street with her brother. They walked in silence, giving full attention to the rhythm of their pace, and so close to each other that their arms and thighs appeared to have fused together. By shortening his stride, Ahnu was able to follow her lead.

As they walked, they drew the attention of those who passed them along the way, not because of their distinct manner of walking but because of their youthful beauty. The long, elegant neck and high cheekbones of Carma accentuated the inquisitiveness of her vibrant, almond-shaped eyes, while the commanding, though gangly, stature of Ahnu, along with his handsome features, could have gained him an advantage in the eyes of others had he an understanding of visual attraction.

The two reached the end of the road and followed a footpath to the river. Without finding a trace of the beggars, they turned back and walked home, disappointed. The tall buildings that lined the streets formed endless walls, winding along like serpents. When the two came within sight of their home, Ahnu's feet began dragging on the narrow, well-worn cobbles. Abruptly, he stopped walking.

"What is it?" asked his sister.

He turned to her and said, "When I first realized that my childhood friend Ram did not exist, I felt like I'd lost something I never had." He let go of her hand. "I am having that same feeling now in regards to the one who replaced him in my trust."

"He exists," she replied curtly. "This is certain."

"Part of me believes that but another part of me doubts it. How can you be so sure?"

"Because I experienced the very truth of his words for myself," she said, forthright.

After pondering her remark, he said, "Ram often told us, 'To know the still mind is all that need be known.' I never questioned his words, but . . . but my mind never remains still for long enough to experience their truth."

"I had the same frustration as you, so I asked him about it," she said. "You remember. Don't you? After I told you what he said, you asked me to repeat it to you several times."

"Will you tell me again?" he asked meekly.

Gazing up at the sky, she mused for a few moments before saying, "He told me the mind is like a whirlwind, constantly spinning thoughts. If I fix my attention on my thoughts as they arise, without engaging in them, I will discover that their origin is where I truly am.

"He had told me this many times before, but in that moment I felt as though I was hearing his guidance for the first time and felt compelled to follow it. In so doing, I became aware that all of my thoughts revolved around one single thought, which was based on the perception I had of myself.

"I noticed this perception appeared and disappeared at random and had absolutely no substance. Whenever I focused on it, it vanished along with the thoughts that were dependent upon it. In this mental stillness, I found myself." A smile swept across her face as she repeated her affirmation. "I experienced the very truth of his words for myself." But her smile left as quickly as it came. "This experience occurred only in his presence."

"Why are you two just standing down there in the street?" yelled their mother from her window on the second floor of the three-story building facing them. Their father's grain store was on the ground floor, and their aunt lived above them on the third floor with her husband and their three daughters.

After the two climbed the staircase, they entered the large central room of their home. The kitchen was on one side of the room and, on the opposite side, a broad window with a balcony overlooked the street. The modest furnishings of the room were dwarfed by a rectangular table, which stood in the center. The large table could easily accommodate eight or more persons, which it often did, because their father was inclined to invite pilgrims and friends from the temple to their home for dinner.

"Where have you been?" asked their mother, anxious.

"You know, Mama. I tell you every day," replied Carma. "We walked through town. Ahnu finds pleasure in being out among people."

"But so much sun is not good for him. Look at his parched complexion," she said, scrutinizing her son's face. "Come with me!"

He grunted obstinately as his mother led him to the kitchen. When he sat down in a chair, she knelt in front of him and unlaced his shoes.

"Oh, my!" she exclaimed, looking at his feet. "Your feet are swollen and as red as my kerchief." She filled a basin with water and placed it on the floor in front of him to wash his feet. Then she turned to her daughter and said firmly, "Tomorrow you two will walk no further than the street in front of our home."

Ahnu stopped breathing and his face began turning a purplish color.

"What's happening to you?" shrieked his mother. Carma ran to her side as her brother stood up and swayed from side to side. "Stop this! You're suffocating me!" he stammered. "You've kept me in a cage all my life." Every part of his body was shaking. "Let me go . . . I beg you, please let me go!"

The mother dropped her head, and her eyes filled with tears. Carma put her arm around her as Ahnu stood before them, trembling. The mother tried to speak but her uncontrollable sobs prevented her. When her tears subsided, she said, "What else can I do? I am your mother and I need to care for you." Then she began sobbing again and buried her face in her hands.

Carma gently touched her mother's shoulder to console her and said, "I'll be back in a moment." Then she led her brother to his small room adjacent to the kitchen, which also served as the pantry. One wall of the room was lined with shelves, laden with jars and staples. Below them stood a bed that touched three walls. When she let go of her brother's arm, he collapsed on the bed, which he had clearly outgrown.

"Are you all right now?" she asked.

Her brother nodded, though he was still trembling. She sat beside him on the bed and gazed out of the diminutive window on the facing wall. When the bed stopped shaking from his tremors, she stood up, opened the window and left the room.

The mother had stopped crying by the time Carma sat down beside her. For a long while, the two women did not speak. The mother broke the silence when she confided, "I drowned my sorrows of your baby sister's passing by giving your brother the attention that I would have given to her. I never stopped treating him as though he were a baby, incapable of caring for himself." She turned to her daughter with a pained expression on her face. "He's right. I have kept him in a cage . . . though I wasn't aware of it. Now he's a grown man, a helpless grown man." She began crying again.

Regaining her composure, she said wistfully, "I've wronged both of my children, not only my son but you as well by not protecting you from your father's abuse. I convinced myself he was an honorable man, since he goes to temple two times each day, and . . . well, he is kind and generous to others. Whenever I speak to him in your defense, he accuses me of spoiling my children." Tears ran down her cheeks, though this time they were not accompanied by anxiety. "I am the one to blame for the misfortunes of my family."

Carma stared soulfully at her mother and said, "And I had thought I was the one to blame for our misfortunes." Her voice softened. "You are not to blame any more than I am . . . or any of us. I've recently come to learn that we are born with tendencies that determine the way we act. How can we blame others or ourselves if we are ignorant of these tendencies?"

While Carma was speaking, her mother wiped her eyes with her kerchief, and the anguished expression left her face. "You'd better hurry off to clean your father's store, dear, before he returns from the temple."

The two women exchanged consoling smiles as Carma stood up to leave.

When the family sat down for their evening meal, a disconcerting silence loomed over the table. Midway through the meal, the father snidely remarked, "Mutton? Have we gained a surplus of money to warrant such luxury?" He directed the question to his daughter. "I imagine you can account for this, and also why each and every one of my customers paid their credit balances in full this week. I certainly couldn't."

He paused and set his fork down. "The old spinster, who lives across from the temple, piqued my interest when she gave me a bag of apples after she paid her balance. I asked her, 'Why such a generous gift?' She replied, 'I'm concerned about the welfare of your family.' I prodded her, 'Concerned?' The spinster smiled compassionately at me and then turned away to leave. But I continued to question her until she told me that she had seen my children sitting among the beggars, taking alms."

Carma appeared unaffected by the implications of his story, though her brother dropped his head and sank down in his chair.

"Do I not provide well enough for my family, *beggar girl*?"

he asked, as his voice rose. "And using your blind brother to assist you—disgraceful! You continue to shame this family." He picked up a potato from his plate and threw it at her.

"That's not true!" cried the mother. Then her words jumbled, and she began babbling like a child.

"I see," said her husband snidely. "You are in cahoots with her."

Ahnu stumbled away from the table, using the wall to guide him to his room, while his sister sat staring at the plate of uneaten food in front of her.

"I should have married you off long ago," ranted her father. "But now, who will marry you? You are nothing but a beggar girl." He began eating his meal again.

Carma stood up.

"Where are you going?" he snapped. "I haven't finished eating yet."

"To read to Ahnu," she calmly replied.

"Not before you clear and wash the dishes," he ordered.

After washing the dishes, Carma entered Ahnu's room and sat next to him on his bed.

"How do you put up with his anger?" he asked, groping for her hand.

"It's his anger, not mine," she replied.

Upon finding her hand, he squeezed it gently. "I've been thinking about what you told me this afternoon. Does awareness of the world disappear when your mind is still?"

After considering his question for a few moments, she said, "I can't answer that for certain. But I notice when my mind is still, I'm not affected by the world as I had been." She frowned, as though searching for words. "And . . . I have a sense that it exists within me, rather than outside."

Ahnu let go of her hand and began fidgeting. With a quiver in his voice, he said, "My imaginary friend Ram was my savior and protector throughout my childhood. When I gave him my full attention, I didn't have to face the weak, dependent, useless person I saw myself to be. He was everything I was not." His voice steadied. "When I first stood in front of the real Ram, I felt I was in the presence of the purest of beings. From that moment forth, I could no longer find my imaginary friend."

"How did this affect you?" she asked, concerned.

"I was terrified. I felt I had lost everything I trusted and believed to be true. But, at the same time, I had a surprising sense of relief." The tension left his voice. "I am aware that my thoughts are overshadowed by one single thought—the perception of who I imagine myself to be—just as you have told me. But when I face this perception, I can't help but turn my attention away because I don't like it. It frightens me."

His sister comforted him by stroking his arm and said, "As you were speaking, I could almost hear Ram asking you, 'Who is the one who turns away?' Then he might say, 'When you realize without a single doubt that your perception is an illusion, you will discover that the one who remains in its absence is who you actually are.'"

"Yes, he often told us that," concurred Ahnu. "Still, I haven't been able to follow his instruction, no matter how hard I try." He paused for a few moments, shaking his head. "I wonder if there is another way for someone like me."

With an empathetic tone in her voice, she replied, "I imagine there are as many ways to the truth as there are seekers of it." She opened her book. "Would you like me to read to you?"

He leaned back and rested his head on his pillow, which was his way of welcoming her offer.

The next morning, the father rose well before sunrise, as was his habit. His wife dutifully made his breakfast, which he hurriedly ate before leaving for the temple. A short while later, Carma came out from her room. Her mother approached her and said, "I'm so sorry about your father's conduct last night." The mother skewed her head and wrinkled her forehead as she looked at her daughter. "But you weren't affected by it. Were you?"

"No," Carma replied dispassionately. "He is the one who suffers and is in need of your condolences, not I."

"You're right," agreed her mother. "Your father suffers terribly. He is generous and compassionate toward others but much too proud to accept their charity or sympathy." She took a few moments to gather her wits and then looked intently into her daughter's eyes. "I have a favor to ask of you, dear. Would you attend to the needs of your brother from now on? For his sake, I feel I should not do it any longer."

"How can I?" asked Carma. "I need to take my nieces to school each morning and watch after the youngest until—"

Before she could finish speaking, her mother interjected, "I'll see that they get to school," and then waited hopefully for her response.

Carma shrugged her shoulders and nodded in compliance.

"Oh, thank you, dear!" exclaimed her mother with a sigh of relief.

When Carma entered her brother's room that morning, he was sitting on the edge of his bed, struggling to put on a shirt. He had put one of his hands into its opposite sleeve, which was inside out, making it impossible for him to continue.

"Praise be!" she exclaimed, surprised to see him attempting to dress himself.

"What are you doing here?" he asked, equally surprised upon hearing her voice.

"I'm your new custodian," she replied in jest.

"You mean—"

"That's right," she said, sitting beside him on the bed. "Mama let you go."

Ahnu pulled his arm out of the shirt and anxiously began telling his sister about the experience he had in the middle of the night. "I woke up feeling as if someone were shaking me." His voice steadied. "When I sat up, I sensed that Ram was in danger, and it was my duty to protect him in the unstable world in which he must live. *But how can I protect him when I cannot even take care of myself?* I asked myself. My answer came in a split second from a voice that said, 'Give Ram your undivided attention, and you will be capable of doing the things he does . . . and more.'"

"And more?" she questioned.

"Protect him!" he exclaimed with confidence. "The messenger continued speaking to me but I didn't hear what he was saying because the Light within me was taking my full attention." He paused for a few moments, reflecting. "I have often experienced such illumination, but never before was I submerged in It." As he spoke, his sister smiled, biting her lip to subdue her emotions. "The moment I sat up in bed last night, my awareness of Ram was even greater than when I was in his physical presence. I have no doubt the Light remained constant as a result of this awareness." The tempo of his speech dropped. "Then, the Light disappeared. I thought I had been dreaming. But when I directed my attention to Ram, It returned . . . just like that!" He accentuated his amazement by throwing his hands up in the air.

"You found your way," she said, rocking back and forth. "Seems like your imaginary friend was your teacher as well as your protector. He taught you how to focus your attention on him just as you are now able to focus on Ram. Ram once said that the most fortunate of us are the ones who can control their wandering minds with single-pointed focus. Do you remember?"

"Yes. I remember. I thought I had that ability when you first told me. But my imaginary friend was a creation of my mind that I was continually changing to suit my needs. The focus that Ram speaks of remains constant."

Carma stopped rocking and looked at her brother. "To be Ram's protector, I imagine you'll need to learn to care for yourself."

"Will you teach me?" he asked, eager.

"With pleasure!" she replied with a lilt in her voice. "But you'll probably need to teach me how to be your teacher. Let's start with this shirt." She took hold of one of his hands and guided it over the collar, sleeves and cuffs, explaining each feature as she went. Then she directed his fingers to the buttons. "This is the part that requires much practice because you will need to align the buttons with their corresponding buttonholes so they line up from top to bottom." Before leaving his room, she demonstrated the buttoning procedure several times, as well as

the way to put on the shirt and make the finishing adjustments.
When she returned at noon to get him for lunch, he was
standing beside the window, dressed in his shirt with all the
buttons aligned. She stared at him with her mouth agape, more
taken by his air of self-confidence than his achievement of dressing
himself.

"Tell me if I'm doing it correctly," he requested while he
unbuttoned the shirt. "Are you watching?"

"Yes, yes," she assured him.

He slipped his hands into the shirtsleeves, buttoned the
buttons and made each of the finishing adjustments as if he had
been dressing himself since childhood.

"Splendid!" she exclaimed, commending him. "Now let's
have lunch." She took hold of his hand.

"No!" he exclaimed, pulling his hand away. "I need to learn
to walk by myself, like Ram does. If you walk in front of me, I'll
sense your presence and follow close behind you."

Agreeing, she positioned herself in front of him and began
walking. He followed her slow, measured pace, placing his
steps behind hers. But before they had reached their destination,
he had stepped on her feet several times, tripped over his own
and then bumped into her, knocking her against the table. She
appeared dismayed by his effort while his prideful grin expressed
the opposite sentiment. Looking at him with a crooked smile, she
said, "Splendid. But next time, I'd prefer to walk at your side."

After Ahnu sat down at the table, Carma left to prepare the
meal. When she returned, she placed a plate of food in front of
him and sat down beside him.

"Until now, I've been cutting up your food and mixing it all
together in a bowl so you could eat it with a spoon," she said.
"Now I'll show you how to eat from a plate, using a knife and
fork to cut the food." He appeared enthusiastic. "I've only seen
Ram eat with his hands, so I imagine you'll want to learn that
more challenging method as well." He expressed even more
zeal.

She placed the knife and fork in his hands, so he could feel their shapes. Then she guided his hands, demonstrating how to hold and use the utensils.

"Use your fork to determine what's on your plate. If the fork passes through the food easily, cut it into pieces by pressing down on it with the side of the fork. If it doesn't, you'll need to cut it with the knife."

"I understand," he said.

But before following her instructions, he set down the knife and fork, and ran his fingers along the rim of the plate. Then he took the potato in his hands and felt it. After setting it down, he pinched off a small piece of it and tasted it. He studied each item on the plate with the same interest. Then he picked up the fork and attempted to eat with it. He cut the potato into pieces, though some were miniscule and others were too big to fit into his mouth. With the peas on the plate, he wasn't so fortunate. Occasionally, he managed to get one or two on his fork. But before the fork reached his mouth, it was empty.

Their mother came out of her bedroom clutching her sewing bag. When she saw her son using a fork to eat, her eyebrows rose. Without speaking, she sat in the chair across from him and began to sew, watching him surreptitiously.

When Carma returned to the table after clearing the plates, her mother said to her, "You'll need to do extra shopping for our meal tonight, dear. Two of your father's friends from the temple will be joining us this evening."

"Who are they?" asked Carma.

"Two elderly brothers whom I met a long time ago," she replied, reflecting. "But that was even before you were born."

"What would you like me to buy?"

"Your father has requested mutton," replied her mother with a glint in her eye.

"Who are these guests to be worthy of such luxury?" Carma mumbled to herself, and then turned to her brother. "Are you ready to go back to your room?"

He didn't respond but remained seated in his chair. After a few moments, he extended his long arm across the table and offered his hand to his mother. His mother's eyes brightened as she placed her hand in his and closed her eyes. A subtle smile erased the frown from her face.

Carma looked forward to the evenings on which guests came to dinner. During those cordial occasions, the family tension was gone, and she saw a side of her father that he rarely revealed to her. He was an engaging and gracious host, at times even humorous. But what she appreciated most about him was the respect he gave her.

Later that afternoon, the mother carried a large box from her bedroom and set it on the table. "Ever since you were a child," she said, "you have taken every leftover scrap of fabric from the clothing I made and sewed them together to form these long, beautiful bands of every color and design." She mused while fingering through the box. "And with these strips of material, you adorn our table every time we have guests. I wonder from where this creative talent of yours has come? Certainly not from me because I wouldn't conceive of doing such things."

"Probably from where everything comes," said Carma blithely.

Her mother looked at her quizzically and asked, "Where could that be?"

"From the unknown, of course."

Her mother nodded. "I'll start preparing the vegetables while you do your magic." She raised her hand dramatically over the table and pronounced, "I beseech you to transform this ugly, drab table into a beautiful work of art!"

Before her mother turned toward the kitchen, Carma had begun sorting through the box. She pulled out most of the bands, eyeing them in different groupings before making a selection. Then she spread out the pieces she chose and neatly folded the others before returning them to the box. Placing the bands of varying widths every which way, she settled on an arrangement of overlapping patterns that pleased her. Then she set cutlery, crockery and glassware before each place and arranged flowers in three vases, placing the tallest in the center and the other two at opposite ends of the table. Her task complete, she moved away from the table to view the finished work.

"Oh my!" gasped her mother, as she stood beside her. "Your table setting is magnificent! Could we be expecting the king and queen?"

"Do you think mutton would please them?" asked Carma, raising her eyebrows. "Let's go make a feast for our royal guests."

Earlier that afternoon, Carma had left her brother in his room with a knife, fork, plate and seven beans so that he could practice eating with utensils. When she entered his room to get some condiments for the meal, he was sitting on a stool, stooped over the plate that he had set on the bed. She watched him practice from the corner of her eye as she removed several jars from the shelves.

"Do you think you will be ready to eat off a plate at dinner tonight?" she asked.

"You tell me," he replied, enthusiastic to show her what he learned.

With one hand, he held the fork flat on the plate and, with the other, he methodically pushed each of the seven beans onto it. When he managed to get all seven beans on the fork, he bent his head a few inches above the plate and opened his mouth. Then, with a quick jerk of his wrist, he launched the beans into his mouth, capturing them all. He sat up straight, retrieved the beans from his mouth and set them back on the plate.

"How did I do?" he asked, proud of his achievement.

She covered her mouth to restrain herself from laughing.

"Well?" he asked, growing uneasy by her silence.

Regaining her calm, she said, "You've mastered the skill. But now you need to learn how to perform it with finesse."

She explained that he needed to bring the fork to his mouth without stooping his head.

"Why?" he asked, confused by her instruction.

"Because that's how it's done."

"Well," he bemoaned, "I guess I won't be ready tonight."

Mulling over his predicament, she asked, "Do you think you can do it using a spoon instead of a fork?"

"I imagine so."

She left the room and returned with a spoon in her hand.

"Practice with this instead of the fork," she said, handing him a spoon. Then she left to help her mother.

After the two women finished preparing the meal, Carma's mother timidly asked, "You're teaching him how to eat by himself, aren't you?"

"Not exactly," said Carma, shaking her head. "I'm only assisting him. He wants to be independent."

"I wonder why he didn't have this desire until now."

"Perhaps it wasn't his time," she answered her mother thoughtfully. "For whatever reason, he is motivated now. And he is a quick learner."

When Carma returned to her brother's room, he was loading the beans onto the spoon with the knife. She scrutinized his progress as he practiced. Though his head was vertical, it was rigid.

"Generally, we tilt our heads down to see what we are doing on our plates," she said, discreetly, "and then we raise our heads back up as we're lifting our forks."

She corrected his form several times, helping him improve his skill. "That's right," she said. "Now you're ready! Tonight you will be able to cut your food on your plate using a knife and fork, and then eat it using a knife and spoon, just like you are doing now."

While she was speaking, they heard their father entering their home with the dinner guests. Carma dashed out of her brother's room and stood by her mother at the head of the table. As the father was escorting the guests into the room, his eyes lit up and his chest rose with pride upon seeing the adorned table. He introduced the guests to his wife and daughter, adding that the two brothers were furniture makers as their father and grandfather had been.

The thinner brother bowed his head respectfully and said,

"That's right. We worked beside our father since we were boys. He taught us everything we know."

His bearded brother nodded and then bent down to look under the adorned table. "This is one of the few rosewood tables our father made!" he exclaimed to his brother, tugging on his arm for him to look as well.

Crouching under the table, the brothers spoke in admiration of their father for the painstaking work that was required to make the bridle joints and carved legs.

The bearded brother rose up and addressed the family, who stood in a row in front of him. "This particular type of rosewood has become prized for its durability." He pushed the fabric aside along with two of the place settings to expose the surface of the table. "Look at the beautiful swirling pattern of its grain." He turned to the father and said, "If you lightly sand the table and rub it with a blend of linseed oil and pine resin, it will look magnificent! Then you won't need to hide it anymore!" He chuckled, though his hosts remained expressionless.

"I appreciate your advice," said the father to appease his guest. "Now, please take your seats so we can serve you."

The father directed the brothers to the two chairs that flanked his at the head of the table while Carma left to get her brother and her mother arranged the table setting back to its original design. When Ahnu stood behind his chair, his father introduced him in a somber tone, "This is my blind son." Although the father remained seated, the brothers sprang up from their chairs to introduce themselves. Ahnu nodded politely in their direction and then sat down beside his mother, who was seated across from her husband at the opposite end of the table. When the brothers resumed their seats, they began talking about a political issue involving the growing number of pilgrims who slept on the temple grounds.

"They shouldn't be allowed to squat there. They make it hard for us townspeople to enjoy the grounds," complained the bearded brother.

"Then it should be our responsibility to find proper hous-

blessing in disguise." The expression on her face became serious. "When my eyes are closed, I get a glimpse of the Light. But when my eyes are open, It is completely gone, as though my sight takes It away."

She leaned back and watched him as he picked up his shoe again. By noon, he had mastered his lacing and knotting skills. In the afternoon, she showed him how to put on the shoes, cinch the laces and tie them in bowknots. While he was practicing, she began writing.

When he heard her pen scratching the paper, he exclaimed, "You're writing again! Writing poetry, aren't you?"

"No. Not poetry. I rewrite the Seer's words over and over again. As I do this, the arrangement of words takes on different configurations, which enables me to understand their meaning more fully."

"Will you read me what you have written?"

She hesitated, looking at him and then turning to the piece of paper in front of her. "I'm not sure it is meant to be understood by anyone other than me."

"Perhaps not," he said. "But still I'd like to hear it."

"Well . . . all right," she said. Holding up the piece of paper, she began reading:

"The five senses interpret the world outside of us.
Inside it is silent.
From those interpretations, the mind creates perceptions.
Inside it is silent.
Perceptions form stories that give birth to individuality.
Inside it is silent.
Individuality elicits the illusion of separation.
Inside it is silent.
Separation from oneself is the cause of suffering.
Inside it is silent.
Suffering is mistaking oneself to be outside of oneself."

He asked her to reread her writing again. After she read it a third time at his request, his face glowed. "If I had sight, I would be inclined to look for myself outside of myself," he said. "That's what you meant when you said my blindness is a blessing in disguise, isn't it?"

"It is," she confirmed. "You are not limited by what you see. Without question, sight is the most commanding of all the senses. Those of us who are blessed with it believe it is the ultimate reality, the holder of truth. We are so bound to this idea that we cannot see beyond its limitations, or rather see what is even closer to us." She sighed as her eyes darted around the ceiling. "Well, such as it is." Then she turned to him with a smile on her face and asked, "So, can you tie a bowknot?"

"Yes," he said proudly and demonstrated what he had learned. "Now I'm ready!"

"Ready?" she asked, curious. "Ready for what?"

"Ready to walk!"

"But you have been walking from here to the table every day."

"I mean outside in the streets. In here, I've memorized the location of things, but I don't have a sense of their presence. In the street, where everything is foreign to me and always changing, I won't be able to rely on my memory." His speech quickened. "Let's go see if Ram has returned!"

She laughed. "Have you forgotten we are restricted to the street in front of our home? Besides, I've been watching for him each time I go to the market square."

In the afternoons that followed, the two walked back and forth on the street in front of their home. She walked a few feet from his side, forewarning him of things above, below or advancing toward him by varying the pitch of her intonations. Though he didn't fall down or collide with anything, he was clumsy and often stumbled.

One afternoon when he was feeling discouraged, he stopped walking and said, "I can't understand how Ram moves about freely."

She looked at him with compassion and replied, "Do you remember what he said when I asked him how he could walk as though he had sight?" She continued without waiting for his response. "He told us that things outside of him come toward him and identify themselves, allowing him to move in relation to them. He doesn't reach out to things. They reach out to him."

"He doesn't reach out to things. They reach out to him," Ahnu repeated several times. "I lack this faith in the unknown. And without it, I am the one who is reaching out. If I didn't limit my trust to what I know, I imagine I would be aware of things coming toward me." For a few moments, he was lost in thought. Then he said, "When I hear your intonations, I anticipate something is ahead of me that I need to identify. If you don't forewarn me, maybe I would have a better chance of developing this sense."

They continued walking a while longer, inching along so slowly that they could have been mistaken for standing still.

When they returned to their home, their mother said to Carma, "Your father has invited guests this evening, so you'll need to do shopping today."

After leaving her brother in his room, she returned to her mother and asked, "Who are the guests? Do you know?"

"Yes. It is one of the cabinetmakers who joined us for dinner last week. He is coming with his son."

"That's strange," said Carma. "Why is he coming again so soon?"

Her mother looked away nervously and her voice dropped. "Because he believes you would be a suitable partner for his son."

"Suitable partner?" questioned Carma tersely. "I won't consider it. So there is no need for them to come this evening."

"I'm afraid you have no choice. Your father has already made an agreement with the cabinetmaker regarding your dowry. You are bound by that agreement."

Despondent, she dropped her argument and asked, "What would you like me to buy?"

That evening when the guests arrived, Carma was sitting beside her brother on his bed. Though she heard them entering, she didn't rush to her mother's side to welcome them, as was her custom.

"You're not hurrying off?" asked Ahnu, surprised yet curious about her behavior. "Could these guests be the cabinetmaker and his son?"

"Carma," called their father tentatively from the other room.

Ahnu took hold of his sister's hand and said, "We had better go."

The two entered the room and stood beside their mother, who was facing her husband and the guests.

"Carma, please welcome our guests," said her father. "I'd like you to meet Yahni. And this is his father, whom you met last week."

She glanced up at the new guest and said, "Pleased to meet you." Then she quickly lowered her head again.

Yahni took a few steps forward and stood directly in front of her. The two were of similar stature, though she was slender and he was robust. His head tilted down with boyish uncertainty, and his voice wavered as he said, "I'm very pleased to meet you as well."

Her father continued the introductions, "And this is my blind son."

Yahni took hold of Ahnu's hand, which was dangling at his side, and said, "I'm very pleased to meet you as well."

The father escorted the guests to the table, which appeared mundane and uninviting without the colorful display of fabric that Carma usually created for such occasions. When Carma led her brother to the chair alongside Yahni, her father exclaimed, "No, Carma! You must sit beside Yahni. Your brother will sit across from you."

As they began eating, the cabinetmaker prodded his son to initiate conversation with his hosts. Yahni attempted to fulfill his father's wishes, but his lack of social skills defeated his efforts.

Ahnu had never once participated in conversation when

guests came to dinner but, in that moment, he brazenly asked, "Did you already know how to ride horses before you began working at the stable?"

Yahni's uneasiness left the moment he began answering the question. "No! I had been taking care of the horses for almost two years before I ever rode one. My job was to clean their stalls." His speech enlivened. "Later, I learned how to groom and feed them. I would bridle them, one at a time, and walk them around the corral, which is a small area perhaps only three times the size of this room. While attending to the horses, I learned each of their temperaments and grew close to them." His enthusiasm captivated his audience, aside from Carma. "One tall, feisty horse became my best friend. We communicated without words or even gestures. Just being in her presence, I understood her needs. Once she held my gaze when I looked into her eyes. In that moment, I sensed she wanted me to ride her. When I asked the stable master for permission, he refused, telling me the horse was much too spirited for me to handle."

"Did you ever ride her?" asked Ahnu, gripped by his narration.

Ahnu's father stared at his son in disbelief, since he had never seen him engage someone in conversation.

Yahni directed his response to Ahnu, as though he were the only one seated at the table. "Just before my tenth birthday, the stable master asked me what gift I would like for the occasion. I told him I wanted nothing more than to ride that horse. Reluctantly, he conceded to my wish, telling me I could sit bareback on the horse while he held the reins and walked her around the corral. I imagine he thought I would slide off of her, which would put an end to my yearning."

When Yahni paused, Ahnu anxiously asked, "Did you slide off?"

"No. She wouldn't let me. At first, she walked slowly, giving me a chance to get my bearings. Then she walked faster, which enabled me to develop a riding posture. When she began trotting, the stable master became concerned for my safety. He yelled at the horse to stop, which she did. But when he let go of the reins to help me dismount, she took off like a bolt of lightning with me on her back, clutching her mane. She jumped over the gate, which was lower than the surrounding railings, and galloped away so fast that when I looked down at the ground below me, I could only see a blur of motion. But I didn't fall. Whenever I was off balance, even slightly, she twisted and turned her body to prevent me from falling. Each time she changed her pace, as she often did, I learned a different riding posture." He paused, reflecting on his memory. "During her instruction, I had aligned myself so closely with her movement that I forgot who I was. Quite honestly, I thought I had become her."

"How long did you ride her?" asked Ahnu. His sister's head turned toward Yahni, though her eyes remained fixed on the plate in front of her, as they had been since she sat down.

"I lost track of time," he replied. "But at one point, the horse returned to the stable and stopped in front of her stall. After I slid down from her back, she lowered her head, allowing me to put my arms around her neck. The stable master came running toward me from the corral. He was frantic and yelled, 'Are you all right?' I assured him that I was fine. Appearing doubtful, he asked, 'Then why are you crying?' I didn't say anything because I didn't know how to explain my tears of happiness."

When Yahni finished telling his story, a lull fell over those seated around the table that seemed to draw them together. The mother broke the silence by asking in a songlike tone, "Did you continue riding this horse?"

"No," Yahni replied. His voice lowered. "When I came to work the next day, she was gone. The stable master told me the owner of the horse had taken her away early that morning. I never saw her again."

After the guests left that evening, the father turned to his family and said, "Yahni is not a pious young man, but he seems to have noble qualities." His wife and son appeared to share his sentiment, but Carma's attention was elsewhere.

During the family meal the next evening, the father said,

"The cabinetmaker came to see me today." Ahnu and his mother stopped eating in anticipation of what he was about to tell them. The father looked at Carma, who was staring at her plate as if she were paralyzed. "The young man is smitten by you, though I can't imagine why. You barely spoke a word or looked at him all evening."

"I'm not interested in being his wife," said Carma without raising her head.

"What do you mean?" her father asked, indignant. "He's a fine young man. He will provide well for you . . . Does he not meet your standards, beggar girl?"

"I have no feeling for him," she said defiantly.

Her father's posture stiffened, as he was not accustomed to hear her talk back to him. "Of course you realize his father and I have already made an agreement regarding your dowry. So if he pursues you, you will be obligated to concede to his wishes, regardless of your own."

Carma looked at her father with contempt in her eyes. Then she burst out crying and ran to her room.

"I don't understand her," he grumbled to his wife. "Any other girl would be grateful to receive such security."

The next afternoon, Carma was sitting beside her brother on his bed when he said, "You write every morning, except today. Why not?"

"Something left me," she said, downhearted. "I feel like the happiness I experienced while sitting beside Ram has been taken away."

"The same is happening to me," he said in a similar tone. "I'm forgetting what I need to remember."

Sullen, they sat without speaking for a while. Then he asked, "Will you read to me what you wrote yesterday?"

She gazed out the window for a few moments without responding. Then she reached for her notebook, which she kept hidden under his mattress and began reading:

"Nothing is in tomorrow
Or recalled from yesterday
That is not born in the moment
While itself is neither born nor dies
It is understood without thought
And is realized as ever true."

After she read it a few more times at his request, they sat silent.

"I am certain that the Light does not diminish in the eye of the moment," he said thoughtfully. "Nor does Ram's presence ever cease to be accessible."

With a sigh, she concurred with him and said, "I have memories of sitting beside him, experiencing indescribable happiness for extended periods of time."

"So why do we distance ourselves from the moment?"

She stared out the window and said, "It's a habit of an active mind; it's a feeling of unworthiness to receive such happiness . . . many obstacles keep me from being here in the moment."

"For me, it is fear," he said. "Fear of letting go of something that cannot be held, or perhaps losing control of it."

In an attempt to lift their spirits, Carma took hold of her brother's hand and said, "Let's go down to the street and walk for a while."

The two had been walking side by side in front of their home each day. Though their pace increased a little each day, Ahnu continued to express frustration for not having an awareness of objects coming toward him. "If I could hold my focus on Ram," he said, "I'm certain I could gain this ability."

"But your walking has improved. So perhaps you are holding that focus without knowing it. I mean, without thinking about it. If you sta—" She abruptly stopped speaking when she looked down the street. "I believe the woman walking toward us is the one whom I frequently saw talking to Ram."

When the woman came near, Carma approached her and

said, "Pardon me. Aren't you friends with the young blind beggar?"

"Why, yes," replied the woman, startled by her question.

"Do you know where he might be?" asked Carma, anxiously.

"Well, not exactly. But I asked one of the beggars recently where his comrades had gone. He told me they were in one of the towns downriver, where an annual festival is about to be celebrated. He seemed certain they would be returning."

"When might that be?"

"I have no idea, but I imagine soon after the festival."

Relieved to hear the news, Carma smiled and thanked her. As the woman walked away, Carma and her brother turned to go home.

"Carma!" called a voice from down the street.

Recognizing the voice, Ahnu exclaimed, "It's Yahni!" His posture lifted in excitement while his sister's slumped in disappointment.

Yahni ran up to them. "I've come to pay you a visit," he said after catching his breath. "Were you both just returning home?"

"We were walking back and forth in the street," replied Carma cordially.

Yahni looked perplexed. "Back and forth?"

"I'm learning to walk on my own without the assistance of others," said Ahnu proudly. "Would you like to come upstairs for some refreshment?"

"Yes! I'd like that," replied Yahni, bright eyed.

When Carma and Ahnu entered their home, their mother was sitting at the table shelling nuts. Surprised to see Yahni following behind them, she jumped up from her chair to welcome their guest. "Please come in. Come in and sit down. I'll prepare some refreshment for you."

"I'll help you, Mama," offered Carma.

"No, no. I can do it myself. I insist you sit down with Yahni and your brother."

Carma sat beside her brother while Yahni seated himself across from her. "You look lovely today," he said, staring at her.

She smiled at him and then lowered her eyes. Unable to find words to begin a conversation, Yahni fidgeted and continued to stare. Once again, Ahnu came to his rescue by asking, "Are the temperaments of horses similar to those of people?"

"Yes. They are similar in that they each have distinct personalities," replied Yahni, relieved to be engaged in conversation.

"Then, is it as difficult for you to be among horses as it is for you to be among people?" asked Ahnu with innocent curiosity.

"Not at all!" exclaimed Yahni. "I am comfortable among horses because they don't expect me to converse or be anyone other than who I am."

"How do you communicate with them?"

"I understand the noises they make. It is a language of its own though they are less inclined to use it than we use ours. They prefer to communicate with physical movements, using their ears, tails, necks and faces. The confident ones also speak with their eyes."

Carma raised her head and looked into Yahni's eyes. He beamed while gazing back into hers.

"Here you are," said the mother, blocking their gaze as she placed a plate of nuts and sliced fruit on the table between them.

Ahnu continued asking him questions about horses while they ate. Though Carma occasionally looked up at Yahni, she didn't say a word. He, on the other hand, never turned his eyes away from her, even while answering Ahnu's questions.

In the days that followed, Yahni appeared in the street when Ahnu and his sister were walking and accompanied them without saying a word. Then he followed them into their home. Carma continued to treat him with indifference while her mother was growing fond of him and went to extremes to make him feel welcome. Ahnu looked to him as a respected teacher, one who could answer all of his questions about horses, which had suddenly become his passion.

One afternoon, Ahnu asked him, "Who helps you with your work at the stable?"

"No one," replied Yahni in a staid voice.

"Well then, who watches over the horses while you are here with us?"

"A neighbor woman has agreed to watch over them in my absence."

As the mother was placing a plate of fruit on the table, she asked, "Do you mean no one is doing your work while you are here?"

"That's right, ma'am. I start cleaning the stalls earlier in the mornings, so I can come here."

"Oh," said the mother with a sigh that expressed both her concern for his welfare and admiration for his devotion to her daughter.

"Why don't you hire someone to help you?" asked Ahnu.

"I have hired many. But they lacked an understanding of horses and treated them with disregard." A lull in their conversation followed his reply.

All of a sudden Ahnu blurted out, "May I work for you?"

Carma looked at her brother in wonderment. In their culture, blind people were considered incapable of performing work and, consequently, were not permitted to take jobs.

Yahni turned to him and said decisively, "Yes. I would welcome that."

"Oh my goodness!" exclaimed the mother. "Would he be safe among such large animals?"

"Trust me, ma'am," replied Yahni. "I will not leave his side while he is with the horses, until he learns how to handle them."

"When can I start?" asked Ahnu, glowing with readiness.

"Tomorrow! I will come here in the morning and take you to the stable."

The mother turned to her daughter and said, "You best go with them, dear, because you will need to accompany your brother in the days to come."

Yahni said to the mother, "You and your husband are most welcome to join us as well."

When Yahni arrived at their home the next morning, the father greeted him at the door while his family stood a distance behind him; his son appeared disheartened, his wife was fidgeting and his daughter had a distant look on her face.

The father stepped into the hallway in front of Yahni. In a hushed voice, he said, "Perhaps you don't realize Ahnu is not capable of doing work and would be a burden to you. For your own good, son, I advise you to reconsider your kind offer."

"I understand, sir. But your son shares the same passion for horses that I have. I believe he will do well, and I'm willing to give him the chance."

The father stared at him for a few moments with a blank expression on his face. Then he conceded by nodding his head and stepped back into the room. Yahni followed him.

"Are you all ready?" asked Yahni eagerly. He noticed the mother had set a large basket on the table. "What do you have in there?"

"I've prepared a lunch for us all to eat," she replied.

"Please allow me to carry it for you," offered Yahni.

She picked up the basket and replied, lighthearted, "Thank you, but we'll manage fine." Then she handed it to her husband.

Yahni led the family through the bustling, winding streets of the town center. As they approached the outskirts of town, the buildings grew smaller and the cobbled streets turned into dirt roads.

"There it is!" shouted Yahni, pointing to the last two buildings of the town that stood in the distance.

As Yahni approached his house, he took the basket from the father and set it on the porch, where his neighbor was sitting in a chair. He exchanged a few words with her and then said to the family, "Allow me to show you around."

A wide, covered breezeway separated the house from the stable. Directly behind the house was a small corral and behind the stable was a large, fenced pasture. As they walked toward the stalls, several horses peeped their heads out from their doorways, appearing happy to see their master.

Yahni led the family into the first stall and said, "I put half of the horses in the pasture to graze early this morning and cleaned their stalls before coming to get you."

The floor of the stall had been swept and was still damp from being scrubbed. The feed bucket and water trough had also been emptied and cleaned.

"It smells so fresh in here," said the mother, surprised.

"That smell is from wood shavings that I use to cover the floor, ma'am," replied Yahni with a prideful grin. "My brother brings a load of them from his shop each week." Then he put his hand on Ahnu's shoulder. "Now I'll take the other six horses to pasture, so you and I can begin cleaning their stalls after lunch. You are going to learn about horses the way I did, from the ground up."

The family watched Yahni put a halter on one of the horses and followed him. Together, they stood outside of the fence as Yahni released one horse after another into the pasture. While leading the last horse, he stopped in front of the family.

"This is the friendliest horse of the lot," he said. "He often acts like a puppy. You would please him if you rubbed his neck."

Initially reluctant to accept his invitation, each of the family members took turns approaching the horse and rubbing his neck. After releasing the horse in the pasture, Yahni escorted them into his one-room house. The unkempt room had only a few pieces of furniture, which included a narrow, unmade bed that stood with its broad side against one wall. A rustic table with a grouping of mismatched stools was positioned in front of a window, which provided a full view of the stalls.

"Please sit down," he said, as he cleared the table of several unwashed dishes and brushed off its surface crumbs with his hand.

"You need someone to care for your house as well as you care for your stable," said the father in jest, though no one laughed or even smiled.

Annoyed by his remark, his wife began bustling around the table, unpacking the basket and telling Carma how she could assist her. During the meal, each of the family members, except Carma, asked Yahni question after question about horses and his work at the stable. As Carma was clearing the table after the meal, her father told her in no uncertain terms, "After you bring your brother here in the mornings, take some time to tidy up this room."

Carma's expression of displeasure prompted Yahni to say, "No. That won't be necessary, sir." He hesitated, realizing he would need to justify himself. "My neighbor has agreed to do that."

Ignoring Yahni's remark, the father continued to glare at his daughter. As she looked around the room, her expression softened, and she nodded complacently. Just before the family left, the father thanked Yahni for his hospitality. Then he turned to his son and said in a perfunctory manner, "Mind his words, son." Ahnu did not respond, as he was not accustomed to hear his father speak to him.

After the family walked away, Yahni took Ahnu by the hand and led him to the stalls. "First, you will need to put on these leather sheaths to protect your legs and shoes from getting dirty," he said, placing a hand on Ahnu's shoulder and prompting him to sit down on a bench between the stalls. After he put a sheath in Ahnu's hands, he helped him strap it onto his leg, all the while explaining the procedure and guiding his fingers. Then he handed him the other sheath and told him to put it on by himself. The sheath kept falling to the ground as Ahnu struggled to strap it onto his leg, but Yahni continued to coach him until he grasped the procedure. Once the task was completed, Yahni prompted him to stand up by taking hold of his arm, and then led him into one of the stalls. All along the way, Ahnu stumbled over clumps of dung.

"First, we need to rake the litter out of this stall," explained Yahni. "After that, we will sweep the floor and then scrub it. When it dries, we'll spread a fresh layer of shavings over the entire floor."

Yahni placed a rake in his hands and told him how to grip it. But before heeding his instruction, Ahnu lifted the rake in the air and slid his fingers down the pole so that he could feel its metal prongs. After familiarizing himself with the tool, he took hold of it as he had been instructed. Appearing anxious to start working, he aimlessly began raking the floor in front of him.

Smiling, Yahni said, "It would be best to begin raking from the corner of the far wall and work your way toward the doorway."

Ahnu handed the rake back to him, extended his arms forward and began walking.

When he made contact with the wall, Yahni exclaimed, "Yes! That's exactly where you need to start."

Ahnu walked around the stall to acquaint himself with the shape of the room. His hands swept over the surface of the walls as he tromped through the dung. From the center of the stall, Yahni oriented him by continuously informing him of his location. After circling the stall several times, Ahnu returned to Yahni's side and groped for the rake. Taking the rake in one hand, Ahnu extended his other hand forward and walked toward the corner of the far wall. Abutting the head of the rake against the wall, he attempted to pull the litter toward him. But he was too weak to pull the weight.

"Use your whole body to do the work, rather than just your arms," instructed Yahni, studying his movements while standing beside him. "Also, you will need to pace yourself. To find your pace, start slowly and gradually exert more energy." Ahnu moved slowly as Yahni continued to correct his form.

When Ahnu had a fair grasp of the task, Yahni left him and went to clean the other stalls. From time to time during the afternoon, he returned to coach him, repeating his guidance in a continuous monologue. Ahnu was enthusiastic to learn and attentive to his instruction, though he barely spoke a word in return. After Yahni finished cleaning all of the other stalls, he returned. Ahnu was sweaty and blackened with dirt, though he had only managed to pull the litter a few feet from the wall.

"Wonderful!" exclaimed Yahni, as he picked up a rake to help him complete the job. "You're learning fast."

Just as they finished raking the litter out of the stall, Carma appeared at the doorway. Looking at her filthy brother, she laughed and exclaimed, "I barely recognize you!"

Yahni stared at her, entranced by her bright smile and high spirits. "He has been working hard," he said in an attempt to justify her brother's appearance. Then he took Ahnu by the hand. "Let's go wash up."

Yahni led him to the washbasin, which was located in the breezeway at the head of the stable. He guided Ahnu's hands around its rim before directing them to the bucket of water sitting on a stool beside it.

"Use this bar of soap to wash your hands," said Yahni while overseeing him. "Then take off your shirt and lean over this basin. I'll pour a pitcher of water over your head, so you can wash the rest of your body." Ahnu heeded his words and proceeded to wash himself. When he finished, Yahni rinsed him off with another pitcher of water. Then he grabbed the well-used towel hanging from a hook on the stable wall and handed it to him so he could dry off. Carma gazed at her bare-chested brother, whose body looked like a skeleton in relation to the muscular build of Yahni.

After Ahnu put on his shirt, he took his sister's hand and they left. He was so exhausted from the work he barely had enough energy to climb the stairs to their home. During dinner, he ate as if he hadn't eaten for days, finishing his meal well before the others. Within moments after swallowing his last bite of food, his head dropped to the table and he fell asleep.

"He's not fit for work," said his father sternly. "Tomorrow he will stay at home."

"No!" exclaimed his wife with such assertion that her husband flinched. "He needs to work."

The next morning, Yahni had just released the horses into the pasture when Ahnu arrived with his sister. Greeting the two, he invited them into his house. "I've prepared Alma ambrosia for you," he said.

"Where do you get it at this time of year?" asked Carma curiously, since the ambrosia was considered an indulgence that was available only during the spring holiday season.

"There is an Alma vine right behind the stable that

provides me with a supply of berries almost all year."

Carma took a sip and exclaimed, "It's delicious! I've been told it's difficult to make Alma ambrosia."

"It is a long process, but not difficult," he replied, delighted that she was initiating a conversation with him.

After they drank the ambrosia, the two men left for the stables while Carma remained in the house. She cleaned the cooking area, swept the floor, shook out the bedding and made the bed. Just before leaving, she set out their lunch.

Meanwhile, Yahni led Ahnu to the tool shed, which was located next to the washbasin in the breezeway. After familiarizing him with many of the tools in it, he handed Ahnu a rake and led him to the first stall. Once inside, he took the rake from Ahnu's hands, set it against the wall and led him back to the shed to get another rake. After bringing the second rake to the stall, they went back to the shed yet another time to take a broom. When they returned to the stall, Yahni said, "Now you go by yourself and bring another broom."

With eagerness, Ahnu walked to the shed, feeling his way along the stable wall. When he returned with a broom in his hand, Yahni left him alone to rake out the stall while he went to clean the others. By noon, Ahnu was exhausted though he had only raked half of the stall. After lunch, Yahni helped him finish the job and then showed him how to sweep the floor, a task that required less effort.

The next day, Yahni was in the pasture when the two arrived. Carma left her brother in the breezeway and went into the house. Upon entering the room, she gazed around it in disbelief. The bed had been made, the floor swept, the dishes washed and the cooking area cleaned. She sat down at the table and looked out the window. For a long while, she watched Yahni teach her brother how to shovel litter from the stalls onto a cart. Then she stood up and looked around the room again. Her eyes settled on a pile of soiled laundry on the floor at the foot of the bed. She walked over to the bed, took off its sheets, gathered up all the laundry and washed it. Before leaving, she hung it outside to dry.

As the three were drinking ambrosia the next morning, Carma said to Yahni, "You need not straighten your house before we come. Please allow me to do that."

"All right," he replied in a manner that revealed his growing affection for her. By her lackadaisical nod, it was evident that she did not share his sentiments. Though she continued to be cordial to him, she was still reluctant to look into his eyes.

In the days that followed, the three made a habit of sitting together around the table to drink ambrosia before beginning their work. Since Yahni was not adept at initiating conversation and Carma was aloof and Ahnu was inclined to keep to himself, these early morning gatherings passed primarily in silence. Yet each of them seemed to welcome the absence of conversation, which had a mysterious effect of deepening their camaraderie.

Ahnu soon learned how to navigate his way around the stable. He also learned all that he needed to know about cleaning stalls, though his contribution to the work was minimal. Each morning on their way to the stable, he walked on his own at a slow pace beside his sister. But by the end of the day, he was so tired that he would reach for her hand shortly after they left. Many weeks passed before he had enough energy to walk home without her assistance, and also stay awake at the dinner table.

As Ahnu and his sister were walking to the stable one morning, he stopped and said, "I've memorized the route, so you probably won't need to accompany me much longer."

Surprised by his remark, she asked, "You mean you have gained the awareness of things coming toward you?"

"No, not yet," he said. "I count steps and sense the different areas we approach by their distinct sounds and the pressure they create in my ears."

They continued walking. After a short while, she stopped and said, "But I like to accompany you and . . . I've been told to clean the house."

"Are you taking a liking to the stable?" he asked tentatively.

"Well, I hadn't thought so, but . . . I guess I am," she said, and then added, "Or maybe it's the ambrosia."

He smiled and said, "Let's hurry. Yahni told me if I get there earlier in the mornings, he will teach me how to lead a horse."

Besides having learned the route to the stable, Ahnu's pace had progressively increased. Although he often stumbled and bumped into people or things along the way, he was so intent on getting to the stable that such obstacles did not slow him down.

As they approached the stable that morning, Yahni waved to them from the breezeway and shouted, "Ahnu! After we drink ambrosia, I'll show you how to lead a horse."

Ahnu's spirits instantly lifted. He had been looking forward to this occasion from the first day he had come to the stable with his family and rubbed the neck of the gentle horse. Since then, he had not touched a horse. Sitting with Yahni and his sister at the table that morning, he drank his cup of ambrosia in a single gulp. Yahni noticed his eagerness and drank his as well, forgoing his courtesy of waiting for Carma to finish her cup. When he stood up to leave, Ahnu quickly followed suit and walked behind him.

Carma continued sipping her cup of ambrosia as she looked out the window at her brother, who stood motionless watching Yahni halter one of the horses. When the horse was haltered, Yahni handed him the lead rope and reminded him of the instructions he had given him several times.

"Remember now, approach the horse slowly and with confidence. When you are at her side, rub her nose and tell her you are going to take her to pasture."

Raring to touch the horse, Ahnu stepped forward and groped for her nose. His jerky movements startled the horse, causing her to step away and raise her head. Ahnu extended his arms and lunged straight toward her, but she avoided his approach by stepping sideways. Without hesitating, Yahni grabbed the lead from his hand and steadied the horse. Ahnu dropped his head along with his shoulders in despair.

When the horse was calm, Yahni turned to him and said reassuringly, "We learn from our mistakes. This experience has helped you understand the nature of horses. As you just noticed, horses react differently than we do. They are prey animals while humans, in their eyes, are predators. For this reason, we can easily frighten them."

"These big, powerful animals are afraid of us?" asked Ahnu, surprised.

"Yes. They have an inborn fear of us and are conditioned to flee when we startle them, or when they sense they are in danger. But as you might have noticed, they don't move away in a straight line, as we are inclined to do."

"How should I have approached her?" asked Ahnu, eager to learn.

"Calmly, while reassuring her you are not a threat."

Ahnu appeared puzzled. "You mean she understands our language?"

"Not so much the words themselves, but the intent behind them, which they detect in the tone of your voice," Yahni explained. "Horses are herd animals. Watching them as they interact together tells us much about their behavior and the hierarchy of the herd. The dominant horse holds a position of leadership and is respected by the others. For example, when the dominant horse moves toward an area where other horses are grazing, they will step aside. However, if one of them does not move away, the two will have a confrontation in which they might bare their teeth or rear their heads. The first horse to move his feet submits to the horse that holds his ground. Just now you moved your feet toward the horse when she moved away. In so doing, you told her you are not dominant. Consequently, she will not follow your lead. For us to have a good relationship with a horse, we must maintain a position of dominance."

"How can we dominate an animal that is many times bigger and stronger than we are?" asked Ahnu, disconcerted.

"Among horses, dominance is not measured by physical strength and size but by inner strength. If it were otherwise, we wouldn't be able to lead them. It just so happens that the smallest stallion of our group of horses here holds the dominant position."

Yahni handed him the lead rope and said, "Are you ready to give it another try?"

Ahnu's spirits lifted as he took hold of the rope. He inched his way toward the horse while speaking softly to her. Her body stiffened as if she was prepared to flee at any moment, but she didn't move. When he touched her nose, she stared at him with eyes that grew larger.

"Good," said Yahni in a hushed voice. "Now, lead her to pasture. I'll stay right by your side."

Full of vigor, Ahnu began walking the horse. Each time he stumbled, the horse threw her head back, so he walked slower.

"If she rears her head like that, apply pres—" Yahni began to say before realizing Ahnu had stopped several paces behind him. He had forgotten that Ahnu often did not hear others when he was concentrating on what he was doing.

Yahni went beside him and began again. "If she rears her head, be firm with her by holding the lead rope taut. When she submits to you by lowering her head, praise her and slacken the lead."

"How will I know when she lowers her head?" asked Ahnu.

"You will get a sense of her reactions by the tension in the lead rope."

Ahnu nodded and began walking with a deliberate pace to avoid stumbling. Whenever the horse reared her head, he stopped and held the lead taut until she dropped her head. Then he resumed walking. Though the horse was not accustomed to pausing so often while being put to pasture, she was exceptionally calm when Yahni removed her halter.

In the mornings that followed, Ahnu and his sister arrived at the stable much earlier than usual. From the breezeway, Carma watched her brother lead the horses to pasture, one at a time, while Yahni accompanied him. When he finished, the three went into the house to drink ambrosia. From time to time, Ahnu interrupted their silent communion by asking Yahni questions about the behavior of one horse or another. Yahni answered him like a conscientious teacher. After the two finished eating lunch each day, they stood just outside the pasture fence where Yahni shared his sight with Ahnu by describing to him in great detail what each of the horses was doing and how they were interacting.

Gaining strength and stamina by the day, Ahnu was soon able to clean one stall completely in the morning and another in the afternoon. From then on, his working speed progressed rapidly. He also began walking home alone without needing Carma to fetch him. Though he occasionally wandered astray, people who were accustomed to seeing him pass by each day took the liberty to point him in the right direction. His parents were in wonder of his transformation. But they did not praise him or ask about his work because they knew he wasn't apt to respond. In the evenings, Carma read a book to him about horses, which Yahni had lent him.

Before she began reading to him one night, Ahnu lamented, "My mind is becoming ever more restless: wanting, not wanting, becoming impatient, anxious."

Commiserating with him, she said, "Mine too has become like a wild horse that can't be controlled. I've lost the peace of mind I had known for only a short time, even though I know for certain that it cannot be lost because it is my very nature."

"Wild horse," he repeated. "The wild horse that cannot be controlled. We turned to Ram for salvation because the horse within us was not wild in his presence."

Carma concurred with him before saying, "I was at the marketplace this afternoon and saw the woman who used to visit Ram. You remember, the one who told us he would be returning soon." When he nodded, she continued. "I asked her if she had learned anything more about his whereabouts. She said the beggar with whom she had spoken a while back told her that his comrades remained in that town. Then she told me her brother was planning to visit there in a few days. And, after much cajoling, he agreed to take her with him."

"Did you ask her if we could accompany them?" he asked, hopeful.

"I did," she said. "The woman wasn't receptive to my request because she was afraid if she asked her brother, he would back out of his offer altogether. But she promised when she

returned next week, she would tell me where Ram can be found."
She paused, and the tone of her voice became serious. "When
she tells me where he is, I am going there and never returning
home again." She paused again. "I have no choice. When I was
in Ram's presence, I knew happiness as I have never known.
Every day that has passed since then, I get further and further
away from it. I feel like I am falling into a deep black hole."

"We'll go together," her brother said without hesitation. "If I
can be in his presence again, I'm certain I'll experience the Light
as it is: continuous." Then he added with an air of boldness,
"And now I've gained the strength to protect him."

"But what about the stable and your love of horses?" she
asked. "Are you willing to let go of all that?"

"You said you have no choice. Do you think I do?" he asked,
surprised by her question. "It won't be easy to leave Yahni and
the horses. That's for sure." His face brightened. "Just yesterday,
he told me that if I clean half of the stalls before noon, he will
teach me how to groom the horses and . . . " He paused to take
a breath. "And after I learn that, he will teach me how to ride
them!"

"Ride them? How wonderful!" she exclaimed. "Are you
close to achieving that?"

"I am already cleaning half the stalls, though it usually takes
me all day," he said with a pensive frown. "But if I get there at
sunrise, I believe I can do it by noon!" He leaned toward her.
"Would it be all right if I left without you in the mornings?"

"That won't be necessary," she said decisively. "I'll get up
early as well, so we can still go together." Her eyebrows rose. "I
wonder if our father will start getting up even earlier to uphold
his position of being first to rise?"

When Ahnu arrived at the stable with his sister at dawn the
next morning, he asked Yahni, "Can I start cleaning the stalls
right away?"

Granting his request, Yahni led the horses to pasture without
him. While he was walking toward the house after completing
the task, he noticed that Ahnu had already begun cleaning the

second stall. Carma was sweeping the floor when he entered the room. He poured two glasses of ambrosia and set them on the table.

"Your brother wanted to continue working rather than join us today," he said.

Carma set the broom down and walked over to the table. "He's determined to clean half the stalls before noon," she said, sitting down across from him.

"At the pace he's going, he is certain to do that."

She smiled and gazed out of the window at the stalls. "You and your stable have been a godsend to him."

"And he has been a godsend to the stable . . . as you have been to me," he said affectionately. His calm, candid response surprised her, as well as himself.

"Oh," she said nervously, as though searching for words. "Cleaning your house is the least I can do in gratitude for all that you have done for my brother."

In his infatuation, he didn't hear her response and said, "Each time I come into this house, I sense you are still here . . . because you never leave my heart."

He appeared proud of having boldly expressed his feelings, whereas she appeared bewildered by them. Not knowing how to respond, she looked at him with a crooked smile and then fixed her gaze outside of the window. That morning, she finished drinking her ambrosia much sooner than usual. After he left her, she hurriedly did her work and then dashed away.

By noon, Ahnu had cleaned half the stalls. Yahni kept his word and taught him how to groom horses that very afternoon. When they finished eating lunch, Yahni haltered one of the horses in the pasture and then handed the lead rope to Ahnu saying, "I find it best to walk the horses around the corral a few times before grooming them."

Yahni directed Ahnu and the horse he was leading toward the corral. Stopping in front of the gate, Yahni guided Ahnu's hands while explaining how to tie the rope to the fence and how to open the gate.

Upon entering the enclosure, Yahni took the lead rope from him and said, "Take some time to become familiar with the corral."

Ahnu circled the area several times, feeling his way along the fence, and returned to Yahni's side. Then he confidently took hold of the lead rope, which Yahni was holding, and walked the horse around the corral.

"Now tie the rope to the fence to the right of you, so you can begin grooming her," said Yahni, before placing a bench alongside the horse and organizing the grooming tools on it. "I stand on this bench to reach the backs of the tall horses, which I don't imagine you'll need to do with your long reach."

He handed Ahnu a square currycomb with several rows of wooden teeth. "This is the first tool you will use to groom the horses. It is only used for their bodies because it would be too coarse for their faces and legs."

After Ahnu examined the brush by touch, Yahni guided his hand, showing him how to hold and use it. "Begin at the neck and move your hand in a circular pattern while pushing deeply into the horse's coat. Comb against the grain of her coat to loosen caked dirt and embedded hair."

He let go of Ahnu's hand but continued to instruct him. "You'll need to push down much harder than that."

"Won't that hurt her?" asked Ahnu, concerned.

"On the contrary, horses appreciate being groomed in this way. While you are moving your hand in circles, rest your other hand on her just behind where you are working. This comforts her by telling her where you are in relation to the direction you are moving."

As Ahnu worked his way around the horse, Yahni continued speaking to him. By the time he finished grooming her neck on the opposite side from where he started, sweat was dripping from his forehead and his shirt was soaked.

"Are you all right?" asked Yahni, noticing a troubled expression on his face.

Ahnu appeared to have not heard his question and asked

candidly, "How often do you groom the horses?"

"Every day. The horses would be disappointed if I let a day slip by. Besides, the work is harder if I skip a day."

"You mean you have been cleaning all the stalls, grooming all the horses and doing all the other work that needs to be done here every day by yourself?" asked Ahnu, astounded.

"Alone? Not anymore, not since you have come," said Yahni with a smile in his voice. "But even when I did it by myself, I didn't think of it as work. It is what I have been given to do. These horses are happy; and when they are happy, so am I."

Yahni taught him how to use the finishing brush to whisk off the remaining dust and hair from the horse's coat, and how to use the metal spike to clean her hoofs. After the horse was completely groomed, they led her back to the pasture and brought another horse to the corral. Under Yahni's watchful eye and continual instructions, Ahnu groomed that horse while Yahni managed to groom all the others, one after the next, beside him.

The next morning, Ahnu rejoined the others in their silent communion. By midafternoon, he had cleaned half of the stalls, and by the end of the day, he had groomed the same two horses he groomed the day before. His new routine remained the same for many days thereafter.

As Yahni and Ahnu were walking toward the pasture one afternoon, Yahni grabbed hold of Ahnu's arm and exclaimed, "I can't believe what I'm seeing! One of the horses you groom each day is waiting for you at the gate." When they went beside the horse, Yahni said, "You are ready to halter the horses by yourself, and I have a feeling this one is going to show you how to do it."

Yahni explained the haltering process while guiding Ahnu's hands through the motions. Then he took the halter off the horse, handed it to Ahnu and said, "Now you do it by yourself."

Holding the halter in one hand, Ahnu felt the horse's head with his other before placing the halter around her nose. The horse accommodated him by holding her head steady. As he was pulling up the halter, it turned to one side, preventing him from looping it over her ears. The horse assisted him by turning and lowering her head directly toward him so that he could feel the twisted rope and easily make the adjustment.

"She did! She actually helped you put it on," said Yahni, surprised. "I do believe I no longer need to accompany you as you lead the horses. You can start tomorrow morning by leading half of them to pasture by yourself."

Ahnu smiled and his chest lifted with pride.

That evening after dinner, Carma entered Ahnu's room in a dither. "It's been well over two weeks since I last spoke to the woman at the market square. I've been going there almost every day, but I haven't seen a trace of her. I wonder if she came back? Maybe she's sick." She paced around the room, continuing to babble. "I want so desperately to be in Ram's presence again." She paused, becoming frustrated. "Mama constantly nags me, telling me I need to be more accommodating to Yahni, and she gets angry every time I tell her I'd rather die than be his wife. She is very fond of him."

She sighed and sat down on the bed beside him.

He hesitated before asking, "Are your troubles outside of you?"

"No," she replied. "They go no further than my mind. I know that well enough, but I'm trapped in them. What am I to do?"

"If they are not outside of you, there is nothing you need to do. Nothing at all."

"Nothing," she repeated with sadness in her voice. "Nothing but remain trapped in them."

"Do we get trapped in our stories?" he asked, thoughtful. "Or, are we just unwilling to let them go?"

Carma closed her eyes and muttered to herself, "Who is unwilling to let them go?" For a long while, she sat by his side with her eyes closed. She touched his hand before leaving the room.

The next afternoon, Ahnu led each of the two horses to the corral by himself. If he veered off course while leading them, as he often did, they would nudge him in the right direction.

Later that day, Ahnu asked his teacher, "They know I'm blind, don't they?"

"Yes. They are keenly aware of such things. What surprises me while watching you interact with them is their eagerness to guide you; yet, at the same time, they respond to you as the dominant one. This goes against their instincts. I'll be curious to observe their behavior when you begin to ride them."

"Ride them?" repeated Ahnu, raising his voice. "When will that be?"

Yahni looked off into the distance and said, "Soon . . . I imagine very soon."

The next morning after the three drank ambrosia together, they parted ways to begin their work. From time to time, Yahni came out of the stall he was cleaning and looked toward the house with an expression of uncertainty on his face. A few times, he began walking toward the house but stopped abruptly and turned back. Later that morning, he came out of the stall with a determined look on his face. Within moments, he began walking toward the house with an unbroken pace. Carma was making his bed when he entered the room. He walked behind her and stood motionless. When she turned around, she jumped in surprise.

"Oh!" she said, catching her breath. "You startled me. What is it? Why are you looking at me like that?"

"Carma," he said, with a bright smile and a song in his voice. "I love you and I want you to be my wife."

"I can't marry you," she yelled, panicked. "I love another."

He froze in place, stunned by her outburst. Carma ran out of the room crying, leaving the door open behind her. In a fog, Yahni wandered back to the stall. During lunch, Ahnu did not suspect that his teacher was troubled by the uneaten food on his plate or his silence, which was common between them.

Carma did not visit her brother after dinner that evening nor did she accompany him to the stable the next morning. During lunch that day, Yahni redefined his relationship with Ahnu by asking him, "The dream I had of your sister being my wife and the mother of my children was just a dream, wasn't it?"

At first, Ahnu was confused by Yahni's question and did not know how to respond. Then, as though struck by a thunderbolt,

the person I imagined myself to be. In Yahni's presence, I have been led back to Ram."

Appearing surprised by his remark, she said, "That's strange. The relation I have with Yahni takes me in the opposite direction—away from Ram."

"How can that be?" he questioned. "Yahni is well aware of the Light."

"Why do you say this?" she asked, skeptical.

"Yesterday while we were eating lunch, he told me about something that had saddened him. But before we finished eating, that feeling seemed to have completely left him. His acceptance of the situation led me to reflect on his behavior. He tends to be content with whatever he is given, whether he desires it or not."

"I wonder how that came to be?" she asked, taken aback by his comment.

"I imagine the horses have the same effect on him as they have on me. While you were telling me about Ram's death, I envisioned Ram entering Yahni's body a while ago."

"That's not possible," she said, flatly. "Ram has been freed from birth. Of that I am certain."

She sat up straight, took a few deep breaths and touched her brother's hand before leaving his room.

The next morning, Ahnu went to the stable alone. After he and Yahni released all of the horses into the pasture, they went into the house to drink ambrosia. While they were sitting together in silence, one of the horses began making a loud noise. Ahnu jumped to his feet and turned toward the door.

"Relax," said Yahni calmly. "One of the mares is in heat and two of the stallions are pursuing her. They can resolve this among themselves without our assistance. The mare will yield to the one that proves his dominance."

Just as Ahnu was sitting down, a gust of wind blew open the door. This time it was Yahni who jumped to his feet. When he went to close the door, Carma appeared in the doorway. Her silhouette glowed in the golden morning light.

Looking at Yahni, she timidly asked, "Am I too late to join you?"

"You could never be too late," he said with a broad smile.

She entered the room and brought a cup for herself to the table. Before sitting down, she rested her hand affectionately on her brother's shoulder for a few moments. He turned in her direction and smiled. Then she sat down and extended her empty cup across the table toward Yahni while looking into his eyes. After he filled her cup, the two held each other's gaze throughout their silent communion. When she finished drinking, the three went their separate ways.

Later that morning, Carma stood in the doorway of the stall in which Yahni was working. Engrossed in his work, he did not notice her until he was about to fling a heap of dung in her direction. Upon seeing her, he dropped his rake and went to her. Without hesitating, he reached for her waist and wrapped his arms around her. He drew her ever closer to his body and then lifted her up. Her feet dangled in midair as she smiled and allured him with her eyes. When he set her down, he leaned forward to kiss her. But she pushed him away and ran out the door, laughing as she went. He dashed after her. Catching hold of her in the field just beyond the stable, they fell together in the tall grass and frolicked as their clothing loosened. Neither of them had ever known or even imagined the course of such intimacy yet, in that moment, they gave full trust to the dictates of their hearts. In the warmth of the morning sun, not a blade of grass could separate them or interrupt their rapture.

In their culture, when a man and a woman first had intimate relations, they were instantaneously wed for life. If either of them breached this unspoken agreement, they would not be permitted to wed again.

At noon, Yahni went to the stall where Ahnu was working to get him for lunch. When they entered the house, Carma was standing beside the table, upon which she had arranged the meal she prepared. Ahnu realized his sister was in the room as he sat down. His face brightened when she informed him that she and his friend had just wed. But a moment later, he appeared apprehensive.

"Mama will take custody of me again," he said, disheartened.

Carma stood beside him and placed her hand on his shoulder to console him.

"Custody?" questioned Yahni, stepping to his other side. "You will live here with us. After all, the stable is as much yours as it is mine, in the eyes of the horses as well as mine." He looked around the room and stared at the bed. "The bed that is here in this room is meant to be yours. It is too narrow for Carma and me. I'll ask my brother to make a larger one for us straight away."

Overcome with joy, Ahnu sprang to his feet. Fumbling as he turned around, he reached out to embrace the newlyweds. For a long while, he held them tightly in his arms without saying a word. Their silent communion continued when they sat down.

Just before they finished eating, Yahni looked out the window. "My brother has come with a load of wood shavings," he said. "I can ask him about the bed right now!" He ran out of the room to meet his brother while Ahnu and his sister remained seated at the table.

"You had a change of heart?" asked Ahnu, tentatively.

"Yes," she replied. "When I thought about what you said last night, I realized the aversion I felt toward Yahni was the opposite of desire, yet not different from it. Ram was free of both of them, like Yahni as you told me. Within that freedom all that is given is accepted with a loving heart." Her voice lowered. "Yahni was given to me."

Just then, Yahni came back into the room.

"He will deliver the bed in two days!" he exclaimed, facing Ahnu. "Then you can move in with us. Let's go help him unload the cart."

That afternoon while Ahnu worked in the stalls, Carma went home to gather up her belongings, and Yahni left with his brother to announce the news to his family. The next day, the two fathers sanded and oiled the table and chairs in the home above the grain store and, in accordance with the dowry agreement, exchanged it with the rustic table and mismatched stools in the house along-side the stable. The mother joined them when they made the delivery to give her daughter the box of fabric remnants.

On the day the new bed arrived, Ahnu did not return to the pantry, where he had spent his entire childhood. As the three sat around the table during the meal that evening, not a word was spoken. Silence was sacred to them, uniting them in ways that words could not. After they finished eating, however, they sat on the porch and spoke fluently, jumping from one topic to another. But even then, silence often found its way into their conversations because they were inclined to resort to it for understanding and solace.

"The first time we drank ambrosia together," said Carma, looking at Yahni. "I didn't speak because I wanted to conceal myself. But to my surprise, silence refused to hide me."

"That's how it was for me when I first sat beside Ram," said Ahnu.

"Ram?" asked Yahni, not having heard that name mentioned until then. When he looked at Carma, she dropped her head. Her reaction piqued his interest.

"Who is Ram?" he asked.

Ahnu appeared anxious to answer his question but hesitated, allowing his sister to respond.

She looked up at Yahni and gave a reply that was notably short of words. "He was a blind beggar who drowned recently in the river."

"Is he the one you loved?" asked Yahni tentatively.

She nodded and whispered, "Yes."

"I loved him, too," blurted her brother. He lowered his voice. "As I'm certain you would have as well, had you known him."

"Will you tell me about him?" asked Yahni.

Ahnu's posture lifted as he said, "He was not burdened by his body or the world outside of him."

"How is that so?" asked Yahni, perplexed.

"He took pleasure in whatever was given to him but desired nothing," answered Ahnu with deliberation. "Also, he did not have a sense of himself as an individual—one who is uniquely distinct from others."

Yahni contemplated his reply and then asked, "Was it that he saw himself in everyone?"

"Yes. That is how it was for him," said Ahnu, taken by Yahni's insightful question. His sister nodded spontaneously but remained silent.

Ahnu continued telling him about Ram's nature, the knowledge he was given about his past lives and the Seer's wisdom.

"Do you remember his past lives well enough to retell them to me?" asked Yahni, hopeful.

"I do," replied Ahnu with an air of confidence.

The next evening after the three gathered on the porch, Ahnu recounted the first of Ram's past lives. Yahni became so absorbed in the narration that he appeared to float in and out of a trance as he listened.

When Ahnu had completed reciting the Seer's wisdom, his sister exclaimed, "You remembered Ram's past life almost verbatim! I could never have done this in such detail and so accurately, even though I was the one who originally told it to you." She touched her brother's hand tenderly. "Several times while you were speaking, I imagined Ram was actually here."

Sitting together on the porch after the evening meals and listening to Ahnu narrate the next in the sequence of Ram's past lives became a ritual for them. Each time he finished, Yahni repeated the Seer's words without questioning them or expressing a desire for further discussion. Carma glowed after each telling while Ahnu appeared to have assumed the serenity of the blind sage he so dearly loved.

On the evening when Ahnu completed telling all of the past lives, Carma said, "Your narrations have reminded me again and again of my essence: eternal existence, awareness and happiness." The tone of her voice dropped. "Yet in my daily life, I forget it because I am rarely content with circumstances as they are, especially those that displease me."

Her brother lowered his voice and spoke to her with compassion, "As you often remind me, you would not be discontent if you made the distinction between the one whose attention goes astray and the one whose attention remains steady."

"I'm certain I would make this distinction if I weren't so addicted to the senseless stories that circle through my mind," she replied, disappointed in herself.

Yahni listened attentively to their conversation as it continued. When it finished, he said, "Clearly, the three of us have not come together by chance. We are on the same journey-less journey of being who we are in the never-changing eye of the moment." He paused briefly, reflecting. "When I first began working among the horses, I experienced the expansive awareness that knows nothing other than happiness, just by being in their presence. I couldn't have explained this experience had you not told me about Ram's past lives because it was only apparent to me in the absence of words. I had no cause to doubt this awareness, or draw conclusions, or form beliefs about it in any way. Without words, awareness has no limitations. 'It knows everything, though it cannot be known by the intellect,' as you said in your narration." He gazed at them for a few moments before continuing. "By simply being in each other's presence, we will not be distracted from this awareness in which Ram forever exists."

Carma looked at her husband with the devotion and affection that he had always shown her and said, "What a blessing to find ourselves in each other, knowing we share the same essence."

Ahnu repeated Yahni's words while turning toward him. "By simply being in the presence of horses, you realized this truth. When I am with the horses, nothing within me asks to be found, understood, questioned or achieved." He paused and his posture relaxed. But within moments, he perked up again and continued. "Initially, words were useful in pointing me toward my essence. But I found that if I held onto them beyond that point, I became entangled in them. My misbelief that I needed to gain some sort of understanding created an imaginary journey that prevented me from being right here, right now."

When he finished speaking, Yahni jumped up and ran into the house. He returned with three cups and the jug of ambrosia. As they drank, not a word interrupted their serenity and time stood still.

When they finished drinking, Carma said cheerfully, "I too would like to learn how to take care of the horses."

"Wonderful!" exclaimed Yahni. "With all of us working together, I'll have time to add a few rooms to the house."

"Can one of them be an enclosed room for bathing?" she asked, heartened.

"Better than that, the first will be a full bathroom, complete with a shower enclosure," replied Yahni. "I will start building it after the celebration of families next week. My brother told me that over one hundred people from our side of the family are planning to come. And with the fifty or so expected from your side, I'll need to dig at least six sanitary pits."

As was the tradition of the time, within one lunar month after a man and woman wed, their extended families came together. The hallowed event had less to do with the newlyweds than the establishment of an alliance between their two families, since families were considered to be the basis of an individual's security, success and happiness. The celebration renewed family ties and expanded family boundaries. Some men came in hopes of broadening their worldly endeavors, or finding suitable partners for their sons, or improving their life circumstances in some other way. Women shared stories about their families, exchanged recipes and unburdened themselves of their secrets to those they trusted. It was a day of merriment in which families brought their favorite dishes to share and musicians came with their instruments to harmonize with each other while everyone sang and danced to their songs.

News of such celebrations spread from one town to the next beside the river as swiftly as the river's current. The occasion drew even the most distant relatives, in terms of location as well as bloodline.

On the day of their family celebration, Yahni and Carma

began the necessary preparations long before dawn in the house beside the stable. The furniture was placed by the walls and was used to support planks that would serve as surfaces for guests to set the food they brought. By the time Yahni and Ahnu went to take the horses to pasture and clean the stalls, Carma had begun adorning the planks with her colorful bands of fabric.

Several ox carts were hired for the day to transport guests from the town center to the stable. By midmorning, the first cart arrived. Yahni stopped work to welcome the arrivals, whereas Ahnu chose to continue cleaning the stalls until they were finished. The swirl of activity and hum of voices increased as people scurried to greet those they knew and introduce themselves to those they did not. When the last group of guests arrived just before noon, everyone except Ahnu gathered together in the field just beyond the stable.

The two fathers of the newlywed couple and an uncle of Yahni's, one of his father's three brothers, stood in the center of the circle and officiated the religious rituals to inaugurate the event. Birdsong could be heard in the surrounding trees as the two fathers and uncle lit the ceremonial torch. Carma's father handed the torch to Yahni's father, who in turn handed it to his brother. The torch was then passed from one person to the next, making its way around the circle and returning to where it started. Then the gathering of families drew so close together that those in the front were less than an arm's reach from the three men standing in the center. Huddled together shoulder to shoulder, everyone swayed from one side to the next in synchronization to the closing call-and-response chant, which was led by the three men:

"We receive Light from each other. We give Light to each other. We praise the eternal Light." Then, in thundering unison, the crowd yelled, "Let us rejoice and be merry!"

Ahnu had just finished cleaning the last stall when the loud finale reverberated through its walls. Concerned that the horses might be frightened, he hurried to the pasture and stood amid them.

Meanwhile, the huddle dispersed and guests began mingling as they spread out their picnic blankets in the field. In the house, a group of women helped Carma organize the platters of food and urns of beverages while, in the corral, musicians tuned their instruments.

When the house became overcrowded, Carma went outside. She spotted her husband among the guests and waved to him. He came to her at once.

"Have you seen Ahnu?" she asked, concerned.

"He's standing in front of the pasture gate. He said he intends to remain there throughout the day to safeguard the horses."

Relieved, she smiled and said, "I should have guessed."

Yahni's attention turned toward a man and woman who were standing alone amid a group of people. The handsome couple was neatly groomed and dressed in clothing that appeared to have been specifically made for the occasion.

"That's my uncle and aunt over there," he said proudly, nodding toward the couple. "When I was born, their family and mine lived together in the same house. Their son and I were born on the very same day. During our childhood, my cousin and I were inseparable and so similar in our ways that people often mistook us for twins. When I was seven, his family moved downriver to live with his grandfather, who had become ill and was unable to care for his seven cows. That very year, my cousin fell from a cliff and died. My uncle and aunt were devastated. In the years that followed, I visited them often. My love for animals began when my uncle taught me how to care for his cows." He paused for a moment while gazing at the couple. "My father once told me how lucky I was to have two sets of parents." He looked at Carma and smiled. "One of the fathers in the circle was yours, the other two were mine."

Carma laughed and asked, "Do they have other children?"

"A daughter by the name of Chandra, who is a few years older than me. She was an ornery child who took pleasure in bullying other children." He took hold of his wife's hand and said, "I'd like you to meet them."

When his uncle and aunt saw the newlyweds approaching them, they were overcome with joy.

Yahni embraced the couple and introduced them to his wife. Then he said, "It's been over three years since we last saw each other."

His uncle took hold of his aunt's hand, and the two gazed at him with adoration. "Even so," replied his uncle, "you have not left our hearts for a moment."

Yahni smiled warmly and rested his hand on his shoulder. "I'd like to show you the horses and the stable."

Moved by their mutual show of affection, Carma linked arms with the aunt and said, "And I would like to show you our house."

The two women looked into each other's smiling eyes and moseyed off, arm in arm, toward the house.

As they walked, Carma asked, "Has your daughter come with you?"

"Yes. We came with Chandra," said the aunt, "though she no longer lives with us. Last year, she moved to town and took a room in a tavern." She stopped walking and her head dropped in shame. "She's become a 'dancer.'"

Women known as dancers were condemned by society for their flagrant behavior and licentious morals. Yet, paradoxically, both men and women were entertained by their erotic performances and compensated them well. The pious believed the parents were the cause of the impurity and often treated them with more contempt than their daughters.

Carma consoled her with an embrace. The aunt's body quivered, as if she were whimpering, though she uttered not a sound. The two stood like a single form, as people swirled around them singing to the music and carrying their plates of food to their picnic blankets.

When the guests finished eating, the musicians began playing traditional melodies to entice them to come into the corral and dance. Ahnu looked like a prince, standing tall just outside the pasture gate while listening to the music. From time to time, one or two of the horses would wander up to him and stretch their necks over his shoulder to observe the festivities, while young women inside the corral stretched their necks to take notice of Ahnu. Three brazen girls approached him and engaged him in conversation, asking him questions about the horses. He enjoyed their amorous play and, like a cavalier, offered each of them a chance to rub the nose of one of the horses.

Carma was bringing a plate of food to her brother when she noticed one of his admirers had already done that. Stopping beside her mother, she said, "It appears your son could have his pick of suitable partners . . . if he were eligible."

When the traditional dancing had come to an end, the musicians played a melody that beckoned Chandra to perform. In anticipation of her performance, people crowded around the perimeter of the corral. They cheered when Chandra threw off her shawl, unfastened her blouse and began dancing in front of them. Her sequined, airy costume and bangles sparkled as the tempo of the music increased. Spellbound by her alluring gyrations, her audience appeared incapable of uttering a sound. After circling the corral several times, she danced toward the pasture fence. She brushed aside Ahnu's admirers and swirled in front of him with seductive gestures that would cause any man with sight to blush. Her gentle breeze filled with her fragrance ruffled Ahnu's hair as he swooned. Slighted by Chandra, his three admirers returned to the corral. Chandra completed her dance by kneeling at Ahnu's feet, having successfully won his admiration.

The musicians disbanded after her performance, and people began chatting among themselves while refreshing each other's cups with beverages. Chandra was fastening her blouse when Carma came up to her and introduced herself and then her brother. Chandra looked at Carma with piercing eyes as she reached for her shawl, which a young girl had retrieved for her. The young girl looked up at her with admiration while waiting for a response for her kind deed. But she did not even receive a glance from Chandra, whose attention was fixed on Carma.

"I guess we are now cousins by marriage," said Chandra,

fiddling with the baubles that adorned her wavy auburn hair. The two women looked at one another with equal fiery intensity in their eyes, though Chandra's was cunning in nature while Carma's was inquisitive. "My mother told me you created the beautiful tapestries on the tables. I am looking for a seamstress with such creative talent to make my costumes. Might you be interested? I would compensate you well."

Carma laughed and said, "I can only sew fabric remnants together. My mother has yet to teach me the art of making clothing."

Chandra's mother came up to the two young women and took hold of each of their hands. "I am so glad that you two have made acquaintance," she said, smiling.

Carma looked at her husband's aunt and said, "From the beautiful dress you are wearing, I imagine you have the skill to make your daughter's costumes."

Chandra rolled her eyes and said, "Don't fret, Mama. I know better than to ask that of you."

The aunt looked up into the sky, as though contemplating Carma's question and her daughter's response. After a few moments, she looked at Carma and said with a childlike expression on her face, "Yes. Why not? I could do that!" Her response seemed to surprise her even more than her daughter.

Just then, the aunt caught sight of a stout woman in the crowd and gestured for her to join them. When Chandra recognized the woman approaching them, she made a contentious grunt and dashed away.

"Well! I hope I didn't scare off your daughter," said the woman, brushing a wisp of curly blonde hair away from her forehead.

Disregarding her comment, the aunt introduced her to Carma saying, "I'd like you to meet the niece of my great-aunt. Ever since I can remember, she has been the dearest of friends." She looked at the woman fondly. "I haven't seen your mother. Did she not come with you?"

The woman pointed toward a frail old woman sitting on a

bench in the shade of a tree. "Can you see her over there?" she asked, giving the aunt a slight nudge. "She'd be most pleased if you paid her your respects."

The aunt nodded and said, "I'll be back in just a moment."

Watching her walk away, the niece sighed before saying, "I so admire her for having endured the hardships her daughter has put her through."

"Hardships?" asked Carma, curious.

The woman's eyebrows rose. She turned toward Carma and said in a hushed voice, "After my husband died, I lived with her family for several years. During that time, Chandra would became furious whenever her parents expressed their love for each other and did everything imaginable to create rifts between them. But her malicious ploys only seemed to bring her parents closer together, and their love for her did not diminish." She looked over to where Chandra was gallivanting among the musicians. "That girl has a streak of the devil in her."

Puzzled, Carma asked, "Are you saying she finds happiness in taking it away from others?"

With an affirming nod, the woman replied, "Peculiar, isn't it?"

The troubled expression on Carma's face instantly disappeared when the aunt rejoined them. As Yahni and his uncle approached the pasture gate, the three women wandered off, talking together.

"This is Ahnu!" said Yahni introducing him to his uncle. "The horses have taken to him as though he were one of them."

"Is that so?" said the uncle. He took hold of Ahnu's hand. "Will you show me your horses?"

Ahnu proudly led the two men into the pasture and then gestured to the horses. The tallest mare trotted over to him without delay.

"Is this the one you ride?" asked the uncle.

"No, sir," replied Ahnu, taken aback by his question.

"Then which one do you ride?"

"None of them. That is . . . I have yet to be taught to ride."

The uncle looked at the mare standing beside him and said, "This one is bidding to teach you. Would you be willing to accommodate her wishes?"

The grin on Yahni's face broadened as he listened to their conversation. Prompted by his uncle's proposal, he ran and got the bridle that was hanging on the fence.

""But . . . I haven't been taught yet," repeated Ahnu.

"Trust her," said the uncle. "She will teach you everything you need to know."

Yahni placed the bridle in Ahnu's hands and said, "After you bridle her, I'll help you mount."

Elated, Ahnu took the bridle and put it on the horse. Following Yahni's guidance, he stood beside her and placed his left foot in the stirrup that Yahni had created by clasping his fingers together. Ahnu held the reins in one hand and placed his other hand on Yahni's shoulder.

"Now, on the count of three, hoist your body up with your left leg and swing your right leg over her back," instructed Yahni. "Are you ready to give it a try?"

Ahnu nodded, glowing with excitement. On the final count, he jumped up and threw his leg over the horse's back with such force that he slid over her and fell to the ground on the opposite side.

Helping him stand up, the uncle said with deference, "May this be your first and last fall."

Ahnu hurried back to the other side of the horse without wasting a moment. "I'm ready to try again," he said, hopeful.

When he was hoisted up the second time, he landed squarely on top of the horse. Immediately, she began walking forward with Ahnu sitting erect on her back.

The uncle stared at Ahnu riding away and murmured to himself, "He has the selfless makings of a legendary horseman."

"Look at her hold her head high and prance along as if she were carrying a nobleman," said Yahni, bright eyed. "I wonder if his rigid posture is making her overly cautious. Should I tell him to be more at ease?"

"I think I see something moving over there," said Zee, the scrawny one of the three. He grabbed hold of the ringleader's arm. "It must be him."

"Let go of me!" snapped the ringleader, indignant. "Follow him! See where he goes."

When Aja had returned from the hill, he washed his feet in the stream and drank from it. Then he walked to where he usually slept. As he was opening his blanket, the three ruffians sprang from behind him. The ringleader pulled Aja's arms behind his back, Zee snatched the blanket from his hands and the third one scoured the area in hopes of pilfering his things.

"Search him!" commanded the ringleader.

Skittish, Zee rummaged through his clothing. "His pockets are empty!" he said.

In a fit of anger, the ringleader let go of Aja's arms and grabbed hold of his neck. "You worthless, blind idiot! Where do you keep the things people give you?"

"You already have the blanket," said Aja. "That is all I have."

Squeezing his neck so tight that Aja couldn't speak, he demanded, "Tell me!"

"He doesn't have anything!" exclaimed Zee. Fearing the ringleader would kill the blind man, he said in a hushed voice, "I hear people coming! Take this blanket and let's get out of here."

The ringleader pushed Aja to the ground and flung the blanket in his face before racing off behind the other two. Regaining his breath, Aja sat up, dazed, and leaned against a tree. The next morning when the fisherman's sister and the aunt arrived, Aja was still leaning against the tree in the same position he had kept throughout the night.

Not suspecting what had taken place, the sister went before Aja and said, "I have brought you soap, a towel and a fresh change of clothing." Leaning closer to him, she noticed red marks around his neck. "What happened to your neck?"

Aja smiled and extended his hands to receive the things she brought. Then he stood up and went off toward the stream to bathe.

The aunt came beside her and asked with concern, "What is it? What did you see?"

"He had red marks all around his neck," she replied. "I don't think it was a rash or irritation from the sun . . . I don't know what it is, but I'll keep a close watch on it." Her mood became reflective as she gazed toward the stream. "When I enter this beech grove each day, I feel blessed. I don't remember ever having known such joy."

"This is my experience as well," concurred the aunt with a brightening face. "I have been a pious woman all my life, abiding in the rituals and traditions of the temple. The joy I found in the religious life brought me light, like that from a candle. Yet its luminosity is lost in the all-encompassing Light that I find here."

A woman carrying a large bowl of food joined them. Her rosy cheeks and clear blue eyes accentuated her bubbly youthfulness. Having overheard their conversation, she added, "My mother died just before I started coming here. I was certain that I would never again experience such happiness as I had known with her. But each time I enter this grove of trees, I sense she is still alive and sits among us."

Heartened, the aunt smiled at her and said, "Such a big bowl of food you have brought today."

The young woman swayed her head, tossing her thick single braid to and fro. "Do you remember when I first began coming here?" she asked cheerfully. "I would bring him just a small bowl of potage. But since he insisted on sharing it with everyone around him, I've needed to make more and more."

"Indeed!" said the fisherman's sister, laughing. "We're now feeding his flock as well. The noon meal has become a community feast in the woods."

They continued conversing as two other women joined them. But the moment they saw Aja returning from the stream, they all abruptly stopped talking. Those who frequented the beech grove never spoke to one another in Aja's presence, though they had no qualms about speaking to him directly. Newcomers quickly learned the unspoken

He handed her a bottle that she quickly put into her purse. "Show me the way," she ordered. "We must hurry."

When the two came to the center of the grove, Zee slowed his pace, stepping cautiously so as not to make noise. "He should be somewhere around here," he whispered. "There he is! I see him over there."

Chandra strained her eyes to see where he was pointing. When she spotted Aja's silhouette, she said, "Wait here until I return."

She proceeded on her own, creeping along. When she came within several paces of Aja, she stopped and loosened the knot of her shawl. Then she assumed a normal stride and came before him.

"Oh!" she exclaimed, as though frightened upon seeing him. "Who are you? What are you doing here?"

"I might ask the same of you," said Aja.

"I have lost my way in the darkness of the night," she replied, forlorn. "I am going to the temple. Might you show me the way?"

"I'm sorry," he said. "But I'm unable to help you."

"Why?" she asked.

"I am blind."

"Oh," she said, sounding as if her fears were suddenly alleviated.

She sat beside him. "Are you lost out here all by yourself?"

"No. This is where I live."

Sounding concerned, she asked, "Who cares for you?"

"I manage fine by myself," he answered.

"You are so thin. I imagine you aren't eating well," she said, as she unwrapped a piece of cloth that she had taken out from her purse. "I made sweet bread just this morning. I'd be most delighted if you would share this with me."

She placed a morsel of bread in his hand. He held it but did not move. Noticing his hesitation, she guided his hand to his mouth and, with her other hand, caressed the back of his neck. She drew closer to him as he ate, surrounding him with her sweet fragrance while cooing in his ear. When he finished eating, she took the bottle from her purse and brought it to his lips as tenderly as a mother would nurture her baby. After drinking, he teetered from side to side while she spread out her shawl behind them and took off her blouse. Before she disappeared into the night, she had seduced him. She returned the next night and the night after. For a while, her visits were frequent, but then they decreased and finally stopped altogether.

Many months passed before Chandra made her appearance in the beech grove again. Those gathered had just begun eating their noon meal when they heard Zee in the distance. When he approached, Chandra came forth from behind him. He continued playing as she danced in circles around Aja, beguiling him with her gentle breeze of heavenly fragrances and the tinkling sounds of her jewelry, which adorned her arms and ankles.

"Chandra!" yelled her mother. "He is not soliciting your entertainment. Please come over here and have something to eat with us."

Chandra stopped dancing and faced her mother. Those gathered fixed their attention on her as she parted her shawl to reveal her rotund belly. "I have come to take my husband," she said.

"You liar!" shouted a woman from within the group. "He would never touch a filthy thing like you. Leave here at once!" She was about to lunge toward Chandra when her husband grabbed hold of her arm. "You cannot deceive us with your trickery," ranted the woman. "The child you carry has the seed of many men."

Another woman added, "Even if you could prove your claim, we would not believe it."

The fisherman approached Chandra and nudged her in the direction from which she came. "Go!" he commanded. "Leave us in peace."

Zee stepped between him and Chandra and said, "What she says is true. They met by chance one night and he pursued her, not just once but many times thereafter. He is accountable to the woman he has taken and the child she is to bear. You know as well as I that it is his duty to provide for them." He turned his head toward Aja and spoke louder. "He will not deny his responsibility because that would be dishonorable."

The fisherman appeared befuddled. "But he is blind," he said, floundering for words. "He is not capable of working."

"Have you forgotten he is capable of begging?" asked Zee. "Indeed, he *can* provide for her."

"Begging!" exclaimed a man from within the gathering. "He never asks anything of anyone."

"Your accusations are absurd. You cannot prove he is the father," yelled a woman. "You are not welcome here. Go away!"

Chandra gave the woman a cold stare and said, "I will leave . . . with my husband." She casually twirled around and sat beside Aja. Then she wrapped her arms around him and whispered in his ear. The gathering stood aghast, watching her fondle his hair and rub her cheek against his. She took hold of his hand and stood up. At her prodding, he stood up as well.

The two walked away hand in hand while Zee followed behind, playing his flute. The gathering stood paralyzed, as the sounds of whimpering women displaced the fading music of the flute.

"He's abandoned us," cried out one woman.

Another said, "He's deceived us by living an alternate life."

"How is he to be blamed?" argued the man standing beside her. "She trapped him in her wicked ways."

Another man said, "What do you mean? He could have refused her! Is his fortitude weaker than that of the devil herself?"

The silence that had always brought harmony to the group was replaced by anger as they argued among themselves.

A woman yelled out, "It's that evil woman." Then she stood in front of the aunt. "The wrath of your polluted blood is the cause of this."

The aunt looked at her with terror in her eyes as her body began trembling. When her husband ran to her, she pushed him aside and rushed away. He faced the gathering while his eyes darted from one scowling face to the next. His attention held on the fisherman's grief-stricken face. When their eyes met, his friend dropped his head and walked away, leaving him behind.

Some left the beech grove dejected, others enraged. Only a few remained sitting in silence until the end of the day. The man who had appointed himself the duty of straightening up the area came the next morning and completed his chore as though the occurrence of the previous day was just a dream. The fisherman's sister also came with a bowl of food she had prepared for the midday meal. Besides the two, no one else appeared in the beech grove that day.

In the days that followed, people would wander in and out of the grove as if looking for something they had lost. Rarely did they speak to each other but when they did, their conversation centered on Aja.

Wandering through the grove, a woman came upon a man who was standing near where Aja would sit. "Have you seen him?" she asked.

"Yes. Several weeks ago, I saw him sitting among the beggars near the temple," he replied. "But when I approached him, the other beggars surrounded me and would not leave me alone."

"How did he appear to you?" she asked.

"Exactly as he has always been—happy and unaffected by the goings-on around him. Just as we have always seen him," he repeated. "That is except for his clothes, which were shabby. And he has become much leaner."

"I don't imagine she is kind to him."

He grunted, expressing his bitterness. "I've heard she treats him like an animal and, at night, locks him in a shed beside the place where she lives."

The woman shuddered. "Whenever I go to see him, Zee threatens me and chases me off," she grumbled before wandering away.

Following the upheaval in the beech grove, the fisherman isolated himself. He rarely spoke to anyone, aside from telling

"Only if you prepare the meal," he replied, with a twinkle in his eye.

"Mine was not to your liking?" asked the uncle, grinning. When the fisherman came the next evening, the aunt asked, "Did you see Aja today?"

"No!" he responded briskly. "I sat in the beech grove and searched within myself for the source of my imaginings."

During the meal, the aunt said, "The days in the beech grove were the happiest of my life. The harmony and unconditional love that flowed between that silent gathering of people was like a dream come true—one I had imagined but never believed was possible. On the day he walked away from us, I lost faith in everything I believed to be good and true." She sighed wistfully. "Though after you left last night, I realized my dream was just a fantasy because it had a beginning and came to an end. While sitting in the eternal Light that emanates from Aja, I had been holding onto this dream, believing it was real. I imagine I could have spent my entire lifetime sitting there without ever seeking the eternal Light within me." She shook her head, frowning. "I wonder if the deluded ones like me caused him to leave so that we could come to this realization."

"That wouldn't surprise me," said the fisherman. "Perhaps you both would like to join me there tomorrow?"

From their brightened expressions, their acceptance to his invitation did not require words.

"I'll also ask my sister and the other vendors at the market square if they would like to join us," he said before leaving.

When the aunt arrived in the grove the next morning, a man was removing fallen branches from the area where Aja usually sat. Moments later, the fisherman's sister appeared with a bowl of food. Only a few people shared the midday meal, but as the days passed, the gathering steadily grew in number. They came to reclaim the gift that Aja had given them and continued to hold the silence among them as sacred. But after leaving the grove, they often talked to one another.

"I passed by the temple yesterday and saw Aja holding his

son while he was begging," said a woman to her sister as they were leaving the grove. "He is a most devoted father . . . *and* mother. But the infant was so small and listless he hardly looked alive."

"I know. Chandra has no interest in her baby and only nurses him at night," replied her sister with disdain. "A friend of my daughter's and several other women who recently had babies have taken the responsibility upon themselves to suckle the infant during the day."

"I have a feeling Chandra will rid herself of both husband and baby well before her milk runs dry," replied the woman. "I pray she gives Aja back to us."

When the fisherman joined the uncle as they were leaving the grove, he said, "For most of the afternoon, I sat with my eyes closed. Just when I opened them, I was certain Aja was sitting among us."

"He must have been," replied the uncle, "because I had the same experience."

For a while, they walked without talking. "I've heard that Zee beats the beggars he catches stealing from Aja," said the uncle. "And now even his comrades are stealing from him. I suspect they'll soon be warring among themselves." Appearing troubled, he looked at his friend. "I worry about Aja's safety."

"I do as well," replied the fisherman. "But it's best if we let them fight among themselves. If we act too soon, we might make matters worse and put Aja in greater danger. The opportune time will come when we can rescue both him and his son."

The uncle agreed but then frowned. "I always believed that the purpose of my life was to save others from their troubles or, at the very least, do good and be good to them."

His friend gave a hearty laugh and said, "My purpose has been to have others see their errors and shortcomings, so they can do good and be good. Do you think the world would be any less than it is if we abandon our delusions?"

"Our pretentious ideals," added the uncle cynically. "It seems we can best serve others by trusting in our true nature, which is inherently pure, rather than inventing some altruistic motive." He looked off in the distance. " I imagine the purpose of my life is to master humility, like Aja has done."

The fisherman stopped walking when they reached the path leading to his hut. "My sister asked me to tend to our mother this evening," he said. "So I'll leave you here and see you tomorrow afternoon."

The uncle proceeded on his way alone. Upon nearing his house, he saw a man standing on his porch with one arm wrapped around his wife's shoulders and the other arm waving at him. When he recognized the man as his nephew, the two men rushed toward each other and exchanged a warm greeting.

"I have come to steal your wife!" said Yahni, cheerfully.

"Oh?" questioned his uncle, as his wife came beside him.

"Yes," she said with delight. "Carma is about to have a baby, and she has asked for me to assist her."

Yahni added, "A few days ago, Carma's mother became ill and is now bedridden." He turned to his aunt. "She'll be so happy you are coming."

"Let's have something to eat before you go," said the uncle.

"No!" exclaimed Yahni, apprehensive. "We must leave right away. If we delay, the baby might come before we get there."

The aunt ran to the porch to fetch her bag. When she returned, she hugged her husband farewell and departed with her nephew.

During their journey, Yahni asked, "Where are you keeping your cows now? I only saw three in your pasture."

"We had no need for all of them with only the two of us," replied his aunt. "So, we sold the others." She looked away, as though mulling over a concern of hers. After a few moments, her eyes opened wide and her expression brightened. "I can sleep on your front porch!"

Yahni grinned. "That won't be necessary. You will have your own room," he said proudly. "The house has grown since you were there last. We have added three rooms plus another with a bathtub and shower."

"How did you manage to do that along with all your other chores?" she asked, amazed.

"I didn't do it alone," he said. "Carma's brother Ahnu helped me. He also takes care of the horses. Did you meet him during the family celebration?"

"No, but your uncle often speaks of him. He was quite impressed with his horsemanship."

Nearing the stable, Yahni began walking faster and called out to announce their arrival.

Ahnu heard him and came running from the house. "Come quick, Carma's labor has begun," he yelled. "Her water broke shortly after you left this morning!"

The neighbor woman was sitting beside Carma's bed, anxiously wringing her hands, when the three entered the room. Upon seeing them, she sprang up from her chair with an expression of relief on her face. The aunt rushed to Carma's side and began assessing her condition while, at the same time, requested the items that would be needed for the delivery. Yahni and the neighbor hurried off to gather those things while Ahnu sat in the chair beside his sister. By the time they returned, Carma's contractions had intensified.

"Yahni," said his aunt in a hushed voice. "Lie on the bed beside your wife and be affectionate with her. This will help regulate her contractions and speed them up."

Skittish, the neighbor hovered near the door and soon disappeared without saying a word. Ahnu sat erect on the edge of his chair, attentive to the activities taking place before him. With each contraction, Carma wailed and squeezed Yahni's hand, yet the angelic expression on her face never left her. The aunt instructed her to breathe in a measured rhythm and, from time to time, helped her shift the position of her body.

When the baby's head crowned, she said to Carma, "You can stop pushing now, dear." Then she told Yahni to take her place so that he could deliver the baby.

The aunt began vocalizing slow, deep breaths for Carma to follow. When Ahnu and Yahni joined her cadence, the room reverberated with the unified sound, and the baby slid through the birth canal without delay.

"It's a girl!" exclaimed Yahni, bright eyed.

He held his daughter up in the air while marveling at her. Noticing that she was struggling to take her first breath, he brought her close to his chest and exaggerated his breath, hoping to encourage her to fill her lungs. Within moments, she began breathing in a rhythm that mimicked his.

After his aunt delivered the placenta, she handed it to her nephew in exchange for his daughter. She held the baby below the placenta while explaining to him how to cut the umbilical cord. After the cord was cut, she swaddled the baby and handed her back to him.

Yahni gazed at his daughter and said to her, "When I look into your beautiful eyes, I see an old soul with whom I have spent countless lifetimes."

He leaned close to his wife and kissed her before placing their daughter in her arms. Carma cuddled her baby blissfully and, for a few moments, gazed at her face. Then, she passed her back to her husband, gesturing for him to let her brother hold their baby. Ahnu, who had not altered his posture since he sat down, received the infant in his arms as if she were the most delicate of all creations. He tenderly touched her head and began noting her features with his fingertips.

That night, the activities in the house continued into the wee hours. The next morning, Ahnu was first to rise. He went straight to the room where the new arrival was sleeping and stood at the foot of the bed. Yahni was sound asleep beside Carma, who was awake with her baby nestled in her arms.

"Good morning," she said. "Have you come to pay a visit to me or your niece?"

"May I hold her for a few moments before I begin work?"

"Of course, you may!" she replied. "Come over here."

When he knelt down beside her, she handed him the baby. Once again, he touched her head and studied the features of her face with his fingertips. When his finger touched her mouth, her lips began moving and she sucked it. To the baby's displeasure, he pulled his finger away. She fussed until he allowed her to suck on it again. Looking at the expression of delight on her brother's face, Carma laughed so loud that she almost woke her husband.

For the next few days, the aunt took care of the house, prepared the meals and taught Carma how to care for her baby and herself.

On the fourth afternoon of her stay, she said to Carma, "Yahni is able to manage things without me now, so I'll plan to leave in the morning." She smiled pensively. "I imagine my husband is growing weary doing all of our work by himself."

"You are as much a part of our family as any of us," said Carma, melancholy. "I wish we could always be together."

After the evening meal, the family sat on the porch and passed the baby among them. Ahnu beamed when it was his turn to hold her as if that moment were the pinnacle of his day.

Yahni looked at him and said, "If anyone were to see you with this baby in your arms, they would surely think you were her father."

Laughing, Carma agreed with him and Ahnu smiled proudly.

"Ahnu," said the aunt, looking at him intently. "You remind me so much of a young blind man who came to our town a while back. Many of the townspeople are drawn to his free spirit and his contentment with whatever circumstances he is presented."

"Young blind man?" blurted Ahnu while Yahni and Carma stared at her, mystified.

"Yes," said the aunt, surprised by their reaction.

"Would you describe him?" asked Ahnu.

Looking at Ahnu, she said, "Yes, of course." She paused momentarily to gather her thoughts. "I imagine he is about your age but shorter and leaner than you. His name is Aja, but some people refer to him as the blind man who sees, because he moves around without the need of others . . . like you."

Yahni turned to Carma and asked, "Could he be Ram?"

Carma didn't respond but continued staring at his aunt.

"Ram? Who is Ram?" asked the aunt, puzzled.

"The Light?" she questioned.

"Yes. In the Light I become aware of forms as they approach me. They announce themselves by disclosing their size, density and manner of movement. With people and animals, I also become aware of their intentions by variances within the Light, which I imagine are similar to colors."

"Interesting," said the aunt, smiling with admiration. "What can't you see?"

"The superficial appearance of things, chaotic movements and I imagine much more. But to know that I would need eyes that could see."

The two disembarked and followed the road that led to the town. Arriving at the temple just before noon, they found Ram sitting cross-legged on the ground a short distance away from the other beggars. He was holding his son with one arm and begging with the other when they came before him. Ahnu fell to the ground and touched his feet while the aunt remained standing.

"Ahnu! Have you come to save me?" asked Ram with laughter in his voice.

Humbled by his master's clairvoyance, he meekly replied, "Yes, Ram. I have come to take you away from here."

Ahnu sat beside him and began explaining his intention while the aunt anxiously looked around her. She saw Zee sitting outside a tavern with his cohorts and, in the opposite direction, the ringleader standing among his pack of ruffians. Fearing that Zee would approach them if he caught sight of her, she hurried off toward the beech grove without saying a word. The noon meal was about to be served when she arrived. Spotting her husband amid the large gathering, she ran to him and, in a whisper, told him what had transpired. Struck by the urgency of the situation, he jumped up and relayed the information to the others while calling them into action. Within moments, the entire gathering of people began running toward the temple.

Meanwhile, Ahnu had been telling Ram about the stable, the horses, his sister, her husband Yahni and their newborn.

Ram listened attentively while extending his open hand to each passerby.

"You will come with me, won't you?" urged Ahnu.

Ram didn't reply.

Distraught, Ahnu waited for a long while before asking his question again.

Ram replied, "You will save me, but not in the way you are intending."

Appeased by his response, Ahnu asked, "May I hold your son?"

Ram handed him his son, who was bound in a piece of cloth. Holding the infant ever so gently, Ahnu touched his head and then began discerning the baby's features with his fingertips.

"We will teach your son to ride horses," he said, enthusiastically sharing his dream with Ram, who remained silent.

From the tavern, Zee's attention froze on Ram when he saw him pass his son to the man sitting beside him. Until then, Zee had assumed the man was another beggar. He stood on his tiptoes and stretched his neck to see what was taking place. Stepping into the street to get a better view, he saw that the infant had been given to a formidable young man whom he did not know. Suspecting that the stranger was attempting to take possession of his beggar, Zee signaled for his four comrades to join him. Collectively, they began walking toward Ahnu.

All the while, the ringleader had been paying close attention to the events taking place before him. When he saw Zee moving together with his pack, he called to his three comrades.

"Look!" he said, pointing to the pack. "They're all together. This is our chance to take possession of the beggar. Let's rough them up so they'll never want to come near him again." As he began walking, his comrades followed close beside him.

When Zee saw the ringleader and his pack advancing toward them, he called out, "Hurry! I'll grab our beggar while you fend them off."

As the two groups were approaching, Ram told Ahnu in a calm yet commanding voice, "Brace your shoulder against mine and keep a tight hold of the baby."

Ahnu dutifully followed his master's instructions, which foretold him of their imminent danger. All of a sudden, the sound of rustling feet descended upon them.

Being first to reach Ram, Zee crouched down and grabbed hold of him from behind. Within moments, the ringleader appeared, whirling his club in the air and taking aim at Zee's backside. When Ahnu felt Ram being pulled away from his shoulder, he held the infant firm with one arm and wrapped his free hand around the scrawny neck of Zee. With all his might, he yanked Zee toward the ground. The ringleader hurled his club, barely missing Zee. Instead, the club hit Ram's head with such force that he was thrust forward before falling back and collapsing beside Ahnu.

The group from the beech grove howled as they came running toward the scuffle. Seeing the frenzied crowd approach, the ruffians dispersed. With terror in his eyes, the ringleader momentarily stood looking at Ram and the club lying beside him before running away. The magistrate chased after him, while the rest of the group encircled Ram and Ahnu. The fisherman fell to his knees beside Ram and propped him up with his arm while the others, in ever increasing numbers, stood aghast. None of those within the circle had dry eyes, except for Ram, whose eyes were luminous and gave the impression that they could see far beyond what was taking place around them.

In a low yet coherent voice, Ram called for Ahnu.

Speechless, Ahnu answered him by extending his free hand and placing it on Ram's chest.

"I want you to keep my son and raise him as though he were your own."

Ahnu clutched the infant in his arm. His voice wavered with emotion as he promised, "I will. Be assured that—" Ahnu gasped as he felt his master's last breath leave his body.

A radiant smile swept across Ram's face and luminosity emanated from his sightless eyes, becoming so bright that it blinded everyone who was looking into them. The illumination attracted those from afar, who came running to find its source.

When the Light dissipated, the eyes of those gathered had dried and their grief-stricken faces had become as serene as the one they were transfixed by. Blood trickled from a corner of Ram's mouth onto a body that appeared frozen in time. Standing motionless, those gathered searched for him in the silence that had always brought them closest to him.

"Who will bury him?" asked a woman.

"It is for us to do," answered another. "We are his family."

Those gathered in the circle agreed and decided to bury him straightaway in the beech grove. Many people hurried off to get tools and items needed for the ceremony. The flower vendor went to the market square to fetch all of her flowers along with those of another vendor, and the fisherman's sister returned to her house to get fresh clothing for the body. The funeral procession began when the musicians returned with their instruments. Carrying the body in his arms, the fisherman was followed by a column of people that kept growing in length as it ambled along in cadence with the music. When they reached their sanctuary in the beech grove, the music stopped and people began preparing for the ceremony.

As was the custom of the time, corpses were buried in a horizontal position, except for those of saintly souls who were buried upright. Several men began digging a deep yet narrow pit in the place where Ram usually sat. In front of the pit, a carpenter was building an open coffin, which consisted of a small, square platform to which three vertical sides were fastened. When he finished the work, some women attached their handmade tapestries to the inside of the coffin and others lined the sides of the open pit with theirs. Ahnu helped wash and clothe the body while two young mothers fed and tended to his newly-anointed son. After the body was readied, it was seated upright inside the coffin in a cross-legged position. The coffin was then lifted onto a makeshift scaffolding so that everyone would have a clear view of it.

With all arrangements complete, the crowd gathered in front of the body and gazed at the beatific glow that hadn't left its face.

Staring intently at the body, a woman broke the silence when she said, "I always looked for understanding outside of myself. Through your guidance, I learned that true understanding can only be found in the stillness of my being." She stopped speaking to reflect for a few moments. Then her face brightened. "While I was walking here in the procession, I imagined we were bringing you home. But I just now realized you were bringing me home, as you always have—home to the truth within me."

After she spoke, a man said, "I came to you with so many troubles. You told me to give them all to you. When I did this, I realized not one of them existed outside of my mind." His eyes widened and his eyebrows rose. "You freed me from my troubles, as you have now been freed from the burden of your body."

During the ceremony, the uncle and aunt stood behind the others. They were among the few who had not expressed their sentiments. The fisherman, who was standing near the coffin, turned and looked at them with a concerned expression on his face that prodded them to speak. They lowered their eyes, indicating their wish to remain silent.

The fisherman turned back and stared at Ram's body. "I have no parting words to give you," he said. "How could I? In this very moment, I feel your presence even stronger than when you were in your body. You were the blind man who gave me sight. Now you are the Light that fills me."

The body was then covered with a cloth and lowered into the pit. The crowd of people formed a single column, as the musicians began playing melodies reserved for family celebrations, rather than those played for funerals. Everyone passed in front of the pit and tossed handful after handful of flowers into it until it overflowed.

The sun was near setting when the midday meal was served. To the merriment of everyone, the musicians continued to play throughout the festive occasion, though not a word was spoken. After the meal, only a few people remained.

"Ahnu," said the uncle. "Would you like to stay with us for a while before returning to your home?"

"I would like to take my son home now," he replied.

In a hushed voice, the aunt said to her husband, "I'd like to accompany him."

"Very well," agreed her husband enthusiastically. "You both wait here while I put the cows in the barn. When I return, we will all go together."

"Bring a flask of milk for the baby and the things you'll need for the night," she reminded her husband. Smiling, she held up her bag. "I already have mine."

He nodded and left them standing in front of the grave, which had already been covered with a mound of dirt. Up until then, the infant had been unusually docile, rarely making a sound or even opening his eyes. People believed his lack of vitality was due to insufficient nourishment. But suddenly he was full of vigor. With open eyes, he twisted his body and turned his head toward the mound. Ahnu stroked his head and transferred him to his other arm in an attempt to pacify him. But the baby scrunched his face and continued to squirm.

"He wants something," said Ahnu, extending him away from his body and above the mound. "He wants me to set him down here."

The aunt quickly took off her shawl and spread it out over the mound. Then Ahnu set the infant down and removed the cloth that bound him. With a concerned expression on her face, the aunt watched the emaciated infant wobble on his back, struggling to turn over. After much effort, he managed to roll over on his belly and stretch out his limbs. The baby attempted to cling to the earth as Ahnu sat down beside him and placed his hand on his back.

When the uncle returned, he asked, "Are you ready to go?"

"I believe we are ready now," replied Ahnu, having just swaddled his son in the cloth.

During their journey, the uncle and aunt stayed close on either side of Ahnu. Their fondness for him was evident from the attention they gave him.

"Would you like me to hold your son for awhile?" asked the

aunt. From his quick response, she realized that nothing could come between him and his responsibility.

When they reached the house beside the stable, they were dazed from the journey and the turmoil of that afternoon. Yahni threw open the door to greet them and yelled to Carma, "They've all come together!"

Yahni's arm encircled all of them as he led them inside the house. He then stood beside his wife, who was sitting next to the table, nursing her baby. With wonder, they both stared at Ahnu, who was holding the baby and wedged between the uncle and aunt.

Carma skewed her head to see behind them and asked, "Where is Ram?"

"He's dead," replied her brother. His words echoed, as though the room were hollow.

Carma's head dropped and slowly turned away, as the glow left her face like a fading sunset. Only the hooting of an owl could be heard in the silence of the room. Confounded, Yahni looked at his uncle for understanding. His uncle nodded to him and then explained in exacting detail all that had transpired that afternoon, including the sentiments expressed by many of the people during the funeral. While he was conveying the fisherman's words, a faint smile lifted the distressed expression from Carma's face and tears rolled down her cheeks.

When the uncle finished speaking, Carma looked at her brother and said, "Your son is fortunate indeed to have you as his father."

Ahnu knelt in front of her. "He would be all the more fortunate if he could call you his mother."

The quizzical expression on Carma's face quickly turned into a smile and she said, "Let me introduce our son to his sister." She reached out and tenderly stroked the baby's head. Still nursing her daughter, she took the infant in her other arm and cooed to him. "You are certainly longer than your sister, but I'd be surprised if you weigh much more than her."

Yahni went beside his uncle and rested his hand on his shoulder. "The brew of ambrosia beside the stable should be ready by now. Let's transfer it to a jug, so we can celebrate this new addition to our family."

When the two men returned, the others had moved to the porch. Carma was nursing her new son while Ahnu and the aunt were amusing her daughter.

Yahni sat down beside his uncle and said, "I hope you can stay with us for a while. Do you have someone watching over your cows?"

Hastily his uncle replied, "No. We'll need to return home early in the morning."

His wife sighed with resignation as she rocked the baby in her arms.

"You are part of our family, and families need to stay together," said Yahni with a heartfelt tone in his voice. "Carma and I have an idea that I hope you will consider." His eyes brightened and the tempo of his voice quickened. "This property goes far beyond the pasture. We have enough land to build a barn for your cows and a little house beside it for the two of you . . . What do you think?"

The aunt's eyes sparkled with joy, as she pursed her lips to contain her emotions. Yahni looked at his uncle in anticipation of his response.

From the glow of delight on his uncle's face, his acceptance seemed apparent. But as quickly as his expression appeared, it left. "I am deeply moved by your kindness and generosity, but I cannot leave my home, my community, my responsibilities and all that is familiar to me," he said, apologetically. "It's all that I know."

All of a sudden, Ahnu's body jolted with such force that he startled the others. Then his head tilted to one side and, ever so slowly, he began rotating his shoulders in a circular motion. Neither he nor Yahni could have possibly known that he was mirroring the mannerisms of Ram, though the others recognized them immediately. The uncle leaned forward on the end of his chair and stared with amazement at the serene expression on

Ahnu's face. Then he closed his eyes and leaned back in his chair while the others continued to stare at Ahnu, half expecting him to say something.

With his eyes still closed, the uncle exclaimed, "Yes! In my heart, I know what you say is true." He sighed and opened his eyes.

Surprised by her husband's sudden outburst, his wife turned to him and asked, "To whom are you speaking?"

"To Ahnu, of course," he replied, puzzled. "Didn't you hear him?"

"No," she said softly. "What did he say?"

With a grin on his face, the uncle looked at Ahnu. "He said, 'Holding onto the known and all that is familiar prevents the Light from being seen. This is blindness.'"

That night, the last light in the house beside the stable was doused much later than usual. Only the Light remained shining when the Seer said,

Every story passing through the mind has a beginning that meanders from past to future, in a neverending procession that ends where it began, to repeat its themes over and over again, lifetime after lifetime. The one who moves within the procession without holding onto any part of it is forever freed from birth.